Inspector Mason Mysteries

Danube Stations
The File on John Ormond
The Italy Conspiracy

The Swiss Connection

J. D. Mallinson

WESTBOW
PRESS
A DIVISION OF THOMAS NELSON

WestBow Press books may be ordered through booksellers or by contacting:

WestBow Press
A Division of Thomas Nelson
1663 Liberty Drive
Bloomington, IN 47403
www.westbowpress.com
1-(866) 928-1240

Because of the dynamic nature of the Internet, any web addresses or links contained in this book may have changed since publication and may no longer be valid. The views expressed in this work are solely those of the author and do not necessarily reflect the views of the publisher, and the publisher hereby disclaims any responsibility for them.

Any people depicted in stock imagery provided by Thinkstock are models, and such images are being used for illustrative purposes only.

Certain stock imagery © Thinkstock.

ISBN: 978-1-4497-8091-3 (sc)

Library of Congress Control Number: 2012924220

Printed in the United States of America

WestBow Press rev. date: 2/5/2013

Chapter One

At an early hour on the morning of April 12th, a young woman was briskly walking her dog, a lively Irish setter, at the same time striving to keep her beret from floating off in the face of a strong breeze blowing inland from the Irish Sea. She had just rounded the base of Whalley Nab, a steep, wooded promontory overlooking the River Calder, when she came across the body of a man. It was lying at the foot of a steep drop, by a clump of mature rhododendrons sprouting spring buds. In a state of agitation, she hurried on to the center of the picturesque market town, built largely of Yorkshire stone, and entered the police station, a compact building in a narrow side street. Sergeant Roy Wheeldon was just about to clock off from his overnight shift when she confronted him.

"There's the body of a man lying at the foot of the Nab," she spluttered. "I think he may be dead!"

Grumbling inwardly, the police officer switched off his radio, which had been tuned to a pop music station, and rose from his chair. His first thoughts, as he accompanied the young woman to the scene, were of a drug addict who had possibly overdosed, or of some old vagabond who, by quite natural means, had come to

1

the end of his road. Not that they saw many tramps in Whalley, a town steeped in history in the heart of a rich agricultural belt. On reaching the site, after a few minutes' brisk walk, he was surprised to discover the body of a man dressed in hiking gear, whom he estimated to be in his late fifties or early sixties.

"Is he dead?" the young woman asked, rather superfluously.

"As a door nail," Sergeant Wheeldon retorted, accessing his cell phone to ring for an ambulance. "It will be a short while before the medics get here from Blackburn. If you would come back to the station with me now and make a short statement, you will be free to go on your way. Lovely dog you have here, by the way."

The young woman patted the setter affectionately.

"They are beautiful creatures," she said, "but undoubtedly a handful."

"Highly strung, the Irish setter," Wheeldon remarked, adding approvingly, "it will keep you in good trim."

"I do walk him every morning. It's so beautiful on the Nab, and if you climb to the top as I occasionally do, you have a wonderful view over the Calder Valley."

"The best Lancashire countryside," the other assured her, aiming to distract her from her grim discovery with friendly chatter. "In fact, it's the finest scenery in the whole of England, in my opinion. And the beauty of it is, it's relatively unknown and unspoiled. Vacationers head mainly to the coast, the Cotswolds and the Lake District. You can't really blame them. Foreign visitors, especially Americans, tend to stick to a well-worn tourist circuit taking in London, Stratford, York and Edinburgh and not much else. Are you from these parts, Ms. ____?"

"Furlong," she replied. "Ann Furlong. No, I'm not from around here. I moved up here from Wilmslow, Cheshire only last autumn, to teach home economics at the college."

"Stonyhurst?" he enquired, referring to the famous fee-paying school a few miles distant. "Then you made a good move," he replied. "The air up here, a few miles in from the coast, is a real tonic. Cheshire has its attractions too, if rather flat and marshy in places, I imagine."

His brief, if rather biased, homily on the virtues of his home turf, brought them back to the police station, where the young dog-owner signed a statement dictated by the sergeant and typed on a word processor by his administrative assistant, an elderly woman with tightly-permed gray hair. Seeing that the visitor was still a bit shaken by her recent encounter, she offered her a chair and poured fresh coffee.

◆　　◆　　◆

The next day, shortly after breakfast, Inspector George Mason, of Scotland Yard Special Branch, received a telephone call at his hotel in Ripon, a cathedral city where he had been staying in company with his wife Adele. She was on a field trip arising from her course in medieval history at the Open University. They had been visiting famous ruins, including Fountains Abbey and Rievaulx Abbey and were planning to visit castles as a follow-up.

"Enjoying the Yorkshire Dales?" Chief Inspector Bill Harrington genially enquired.

"Can't complain," Mason replied. "Weather's good and the food's tolerable. Wonderful scenery, too."

"Listen, Inspector," his superior said, more urgently. "Something's turned up in Whalley, not all that far from where you are now. The local police have asked for our assistance and I'm wondering, since you're due back in London tomorrow, if you can't make a detour and do a preliminary assessment of the situation. I'm sending Detective Sergeant Alison Aubrey up north on an early train, to gain experience. You could be back in London by nightfall."

George Mason pondered the situation.

"We'll meet her in Leeds around noon," he said, eventually.

"Adele can then drive us to Whalley, drop us off and continue her journey south."

"Sounds good, Inspector. I'll inform Alison that you'll pick her up at Leeds Central."

Replacing the receiver, the detective told Adele of the change of plan. She raised no objection, since they had ample time that day to complete her project by visiting Skipton and Pontefract, both of which had well-preserved medieval castles. Her husband's absence tomorrow would give her a good opportunity to write up her report on the word processor.

The following day, they met with the detective sergeant, as arranged, arriving in Whalley shortly after one o'clock. Sergeant Wheeldon was waiting to greet them.

"Glad you could make it so quickly, Inspector," he said. "My superiors in Preston thought it best if Special Branch came in on the case at an early stage, since there may be an international dimension."

George Mason shook his hand and introduced his young assistant.

"Sergeant Alison Aubrey," he explained. "She'll be assisting me on this case, to broaden her experience."

"Pleased to meet you, Sergeant," Roy Wheeldon said, proffering his hand. "Welcome to our quiet neck of the woods."

"Beautiful countryside," Alison remarked, "from what we've seen of it so far."

The local officer beamed satisfaction.

"The facts of the case so far," he said, "are that the body of a middle-aged male was discovered early yesterday morning by a young schoolteacher walking her dog by Whalley Nab. He was taken by ambulance to the nearest hospital, which is at Blackburn."

"Cause of death?" Mason enquired.

"A broken neck. The autopsy established that he had been dead for approximately fourteen hours. He must have met his death around late afternoon of the preceding day."

"The man's identity?" Alison asked.

"Not much was found on his person," Wheeldon explained, "apart from these three items."

He reached inside a drawer of his desk and produced a small plastic phial, a calling card and a roll of small denomination banknotes. He handed them to the senior detective, who examined them carefully.

"Amlodipine, 10mg tablets," Mason mused aloud. "Issued to one H. Seifert. And there's a reference code."

"That will indicate the pharmacy, I expect," Alison Aubrey opined.

"Blood pressure medication," Roy Wheeldon put in, at once. "My brother-in-law uses the same prescription."

"But the calling card is in a different name," Mason said. "It reads: Heinrich Feldman, M.D., Uferstrasse 219B, Dresden, Saxony, with the letters S.E.D. above the name."

"See what I mean by international implications," the local officer said. "The card was found in the fob pocket of the man's tunic. No wallet or other personal document was recovered."

"He was not a local man?"

"We've already checked the telephone company, the utilities and court records. There is no record of an H. Seifert living in this area."

"A visitor then," Mason said. "Someone taking advantage of your beautiful countryside."

"Could well be," Wheeldon agreed. "He was dressed for hiking and wearing walking shoes. Estimated age around sixty. My assistant here, Molly Eldridge, is just checking local hotels."

"In fact," the competent clerk said, "I've just this minute finished. There have been no room bookings in this area by an H. Seifert. Earlier this morning I checked with the local college, on the off-chance that the man was somehow connected with them. They informed me that they have no staff member, or parent, of that name."

"Sounds like he was just out walking," Mason considered. "Have you found a vehicle?"

Roy Wheeldon shook his head.

"There are regular bus services from Blackburn and Preston," Molly Eldridge said. "I expect he used public transport."

"Oh, and there was this other item recovered from the scene," Roy Wheeldon put in, handing a cuff-link across the desk.

The detective examined it closely.

"The monogram reads R.M.," he said. "This could be significant. Where was it found?"

"Lying on the ground, quite close to the body."

"Evidently not the property of either H. Seifert or Heinrich Feldman," Alison Aubrey figured.

"So where do you go from here?" the local officer asked.

"First off, Sergeant Aubrey and I are going to grab something to eat at one of your local pubs. We haven't had a bite since breakfast."

"I can recommend The Nag's Head on the High Street, just across from Yorkshire Bank," Roy Wheeldon said, with enthusiasm. "They serve food all day."

"In the meantime," the senior detective said, "check with local restaurants for information about a man fitting the deceased's description. I would especially want to know if he had company. He may well have stopped off somewhere for lunch."

"You are suggesting he may have been a member of a local hiking group?" Roy Wheeldon asked.

"This stray cuff-link does rather suggest that he was not alone, unless it bears no relation to the case and came loose from someone completely unconnected, who was recently in that area." He turned the small object over in his hand. "There's not a trace of rust on it, even though it rains frequently hereabouts."

"You're right about that, Inspector," the other said. "I'll get onto it straight away."

"And by the way," Mason said, as a parting shot, "keep the media at arm's length for the time being, until our enquiries are more advanced."

"Will do," the sergeant promised.

The Scotland Yard pair left the police station and soon located The Nag's Head. They sat by the log fire in the lounge bar and ordered a plowman's lunch of Wensleydale cheese, mixed pickles and rye bread.

"Charming little place, Whalley, don't you think, Alison?"

"Very picturesque," came the reply. "But what was that impressive ruin we just passed? I just noticed the arched gateway, but it seemed to extend some distance behind that."

"That is the ruins of the Cistercian Abbey," her colleague informed her. "All that remains after Henry V111 dissolved the monasteries."

"I'm familiar with Benedictines and Franciscans," the young woman said. "But who exactly were the Cistercians?"

"A reform branch of the Benedictines, if my memory serves me right. Founded at some point in the 11th Century. The parish church of St. Mary is even older. It dates from Anglo-Saxon times, before the Norman Conquest. Paulinus himself is said to have preached there."

"Who was...?" Alison playfully enquired.

"A Christian convert from the Roman senatorial class," he informed her.

"This town really has quite a history," Alison exclaimed. "But how come you're so well-informed?"

The senior detective, tucking into cheese and pickled walnuts, said:

"Adele is doing a project on medieval ruins for her degree course. Some of it rubbed off on me. Besides, I grew up not far from here, at Skipton. I know this area and its history quite well.

There's a lot more to it. That steep rise you see in the background is Pendle Hill, long associated with witchcraft. In fact, they still hold covens there every midsummer eve."

"Weren't they persecuted in the old days?"

"They certainly were. They were taken from Pendle to Lancaster Castle, where they were tried and, as likely as not, executed," Mason explained. "That was a long time ago, in the 16th Century."

"Thank God we're more tolerant nowadays," Alison said, between bites.

After they had finished their simple meal, George Mason took his time over a pint of Theakston's Bitter, enjoying the convivial atmosphere of the pub, while his young colleague opted for warm lemon tea.

"There's not a lot more we can do here today," he eventually remarked. "It will take time for the local police force, such as it is, to check the restaurants, and Harrington's expecting us back at the Yard. I suggest we take a closer look at the abbey and the centuries-old Celtic crosses in the churchyard, while we have the opportunity, since I'm still officially on leave until tomorrow. We'll go over to Blackburn later this afternoon and call at the hospital, to get a clearer idea of the deceased and a copy of the autopsy report. There'll be time to catch an evening train back to London. It's a fairly frequent service."

"That's fine with me," Alison replied. "I love to visit old ruins. There's a fine sense of timelessness about them."

Chapter Two

Three days later, George Mason and Alison Aubrey were on their way to Basel. Forensics had traced the reference number on the phial of Amlodipine to a pharmacy in that Swiss border city. They took a mid-morning flight from Gatwick, arriving at their destination early afternoon. The airport bus dropped them centrally, near Mittlere Brucke. Grasping their light luggage, they crossed over the Rhine, took a sharp left turn into Rheingasse, followed by another quick turn into Klingental, a narrow street featuring Hotel Balade, a medium-sized family hotel where rooms had been pre-booked for them. The receptionist bade them register and handed them the keys to adjoining rooms on the first floor. Alison took time to freshen up after the journey, while Mason repaired to the hotel lounge to read the paperback guidebook he had bought at Gatwick Airport. Soon feeling restless, he quit the premises for a short reconnoiter, to stretch his legs and gain his bearings in a strange city.

When his young colleague joined him an hour later, they obtained directions to Marktplatz and set out to locate a pharmacy named Apotheke Ritter. But George Mason, being unfamiliar with his surroundings, missed a turning and led them too far down the left bank of the Rhine, crossing it by a lower bridge. They soon found themselves in Munsterplatz, a compact square fronted by stylish merchants' houses dating from the 17th Century. It was already quite busy with early-season tourists, some of whom seemed drawn to an intriguing structure in the center of the square.

"That must be the Roman well-shaft," George Mason observed, as they strode past. "We'll maybe take a closer look at it later on."

"Why would the Romans sink a shaft here?" Alison asked him.

"To provide water for their legionaries, I imagine," Mason explained. "Basel was a front-line fort in former times, built by the Romans to defend against hostile German tribes to the north and east."

"I expect they had epic battles with those," his young colleague remarked.

"Which they did not always win," Mason informed her. "In fact, they suffered some heavy defeats but prevailed in the end, as they did in Britain after quelling Queen Boadicea's revolt. Arminius alone wiped out three Roman legions at Teutoburg Forest in 9 BC."

"You're a mine of interesting information, George," Alison said, admiringly.

"It's all in the guidebook," he replied dismissively, pausing to consult it briefly and leading them at a firm pace along Freie Strasse towards their intended destination.

Apotheke Ritter was partly obscured by fruit and vegetable stands of the bustling open-air market, but they eventually located it in a row of well-preserved older buildings. The display window, consisting of small panes of dimpled glass, revealed an antique mortar and pestle, tapered glass flasks filled with various brightly-colored liquids and a small set of scales. On entering, they found the interior laid out, by comparison, in the most modern fashion. The proprietor, an elderly gentleman with tufts of white hair sprouting from a balding pink pate, greeted them civilly.

"Kann ich Ihnen bedienen?" he asked.

George Mason, although he knew some German, was not prepared for a lengthy conversation in that language.

"Do you speak English?" he asked.

"A little," the man replied. "What can I do for you?"

The detective handed the small phial across the granite counter. The pharmacist examined it carefully.

"We believe the prescription was filled at these premises," Mason said, "for an H. Seifert. We are police officers from England, investigating a possible crime."

The pharmacist handed back the phial and fixed his watery blue eyes on them.

"You have *identitaet?*" he enquired, dubiously.

George Mason produced a photo ID, which seemed to satisfy the pharmacist, even as he adopted a more guarded attitude.

"It is true that I filled this prescription some time ago for Heini Seifert, to help regulate his blood pressure."

"How long ago would that be?" Alison Aubrey asked.

"It is a two-month supply," came the reply, after consulting his computer records. "It was renewed on March 14th."

"Who wrote the prescription?" Mason wanted to know.

"Why, Heini Seifert wrote it himself. He is, after all, a doctor of medicine."

Alison Aubrey took a step back and gasped in surprise. George Mason merely knit his brows in concentration.

"Did Dr. Seifert practice here in Basel?" he asked.

"Until his retirement two years ago," came the reply.

"Do you know where he practiced?"

"At Klinik Mauser, just off Freie Strasse. They specialize in organ transplants and geriatric care. Dr. Seifert was one of their top specialists. I am surprised Scotland Yard is interested in him. I do hope he is not in any difficulty?"

The detectives exchanged glances, as if by mutual consent deciding not to mention the doctor's untimely death at this point.

"Do you happen to have a record of his address here in Basel," Mason finally asked, "since he was a regular customer?"

"He keeps none in this city," the pharmacist replied. "He travels around a lot, I do know that."

"To England, for example?" Alison Aubrey asked.

"I do believe so. To my knowledge, he has been back here at most about twice a year since his retirement."

"But surely," Mason objected, "he would need his prescription filled more often than that?"

"Amlodipine is a popular medication for blood pressure issues," came the terse reply. "As a medical practitioner himself, he could walk into a pharmacy anywhere to obtain a refill."

"I appreciate that. *Danke vielmals*," George Mason said, employing his best German, as the pair quit the premises and re-emerged into the bright afternoon sunlight. Mingling with the shoppers for a few minutes amid the displays of fresh market produce, they opted for a quick coffee and Danish pastry at a sidewalk cafe, since they had taken no refreshment since the mid-morning flight.

"What do you make of all that?" Mason asked his colleague, the moment they were comfortably seated and had placed their order.

"It was certainly a shock to me," Alison replied, "to learn that Seifert was a medical practitioner. Apart from that, I don't think we learned very much."

"I had a curious impression he was holding something back," her senior said. "Whatever that was, we may or may not find out in due course. At least, for now, we know Dr. Seifert's career details, that he was retired and moved around a great deal. When we have finished our snack, we shall cross the Marktplatz and call in at the Stadthaus – the City Hall – to examine their official records."

"Assuming that he is a native of Basel," Alison countered.

George Mason darted a curious glance in her direction, as he forked a mouthful of pastry and sipped his hot coffee. It seemed to him a given, that the deceased was from Basel.

The administrative staff at the Stadthaus were courteous and helpful, once the Scotland Yard pair had explained their mission. Searching his name in the computerized records, they established that Heini Seifert was entered in the Basel Register of Marriages for the month of July, 1995. At Mason's request, they then produced a duplicate copy of the *Eheschein*, or marriage certificate, for the visitors to peruse.

"His bride's name was Celine Miller," Alison remarked. "And it looks from this document that she came from England."

"It lists her parents' names as John Miller and Betty Miller, of Lancaster, England," her colleague read aloud. "How about that! Lancaster is only about twenty miles from Whalley, where Seifert's body was found."

"I remember you saying, George, that was where that they took the Lancashire witches for trial in the old days."

Mason did not immediately respond. Silent for a few moments and knitting his brows in thought, he eventually said:

"Seifert's own parents are not listed here. I find that very curious."

"Perhaps he was an orphan," Alison suggested. "A war orphan, possibly."

George Mason demurred.

"He was surely not that old, Alison," he said. "Born in 1946, which makes him a bit older than the forensic people at Blackburn estimated."

"He could have been conceived shortly before the end of the war," Alison suggested, "on the other side of the sheets, as they say. And don't forget that at that time there were large numbers of displaced people. Families remained split up for years afterwards, or never re-united."

George Mason gave her an appreciative glance.

"You have an interesting point there, Alison," he agreed. "Seifert may not have known who his parents were; hence his failure to record them on this document, which to my mind is a very significant omission."

"Why don't we ask the assistant here to check the Register of Births?" the younger officer suggested. "It may throw some light on his origins."

They re-approached the young woman who had produced the *Ehescein*. She soon came up with the information that Heini Seifert was not recorded as a Basel birth.

"Could you possibly search the federal register, too," Mason enquired, "in case he was born elsewhere in Switzerland?"

The assistant willingly complied with his request. After several minutes, she announced:

"There is no record of him here either, which means that this person is definitely not a native of Switzerland."

"That's rather interesting," a slightly disappointed George Mason said, pocketing the copy of the marriage certificate. "*Danke vielmals fur die Hilfe.*"

The young woman smiled indulgently at his use of German.

"It is our privilege to help," she amiably replied. "Enjoy your stay in Basel!"

It was by now late-afternoon. The crowd in the Marktplatz outside had thinned considerably and the vendors were beginning to reload their unsold produce, signifying the termination of the street market. George Mason indulged his young colleague's whim to look in the gown shop windows for a while. Perched on a low stone wall, he took the opportunity to smoke one of his small Dutch cigars, while observing the final dismantling of the street market.

"Nice fashions they have here," Alison said, on eventually rejoining him, "if a bit beyond my budget."

"Switzerland is an expensive country," Mason said, "with a high standard of living. It prospered by remaining outside the European Union, while trading with it on advantageous terms."

As he spoke, he led the way out of the square towards Freie Strasse, pausing briefly to watch the boats on the Rhine depart from Schifflande Quay.

"That was a very useful little session at the Stadthaus, George," she remarked, endeavoring to keep up with his firmer stride. "Where are we headed now?"

"I thought we'd pay a quick visit to Klinik Mauser," he replied. "Then call it a day and return to the hotel to rest up for a while. Later on, we'll look up a good restaurant for dinner."

"I'm all for that," Alison eagerly replied.

It took some time for George Mason to locate the clinic from the pharmacist's rather vague directions. Stopping to ask passers-by, he found it eventually in a small, tree-fringed square behind a department store two-thirds of the way down Freie Strasse, quite close to Munsterplatz. Entering through the glass doors, the detectives found themselves in a fairly large reception area, well-carpeted and comfortably furnished. A large tropical fish tank dominated one wall, which Mason thought was intended to divert and possibly soothe anxious patients, of whom less than a handful occupied the plush armchairs, gazing fixedly ahead of them. Presenting themselves with ID at the Reception window with a request to speak with the director, they were invited to take seats and wait a few moments. About ten minutes later, a middle-aged woman dressed in a white surgical coat approached and bade them follow her into her private office.

"Scotland Yard!" she exclaimed, as they introduced themselves. "I've read so many novels featuring English detectives; yet I never for one moment imagined I would be confronted with the real thing."

"We are real enough," George Mason assured her, "if not quite Sherlock Holmes or Lord Peter Whimsey."

The woman appreciated his sense of humor, inviting them to sit down facing her desk.

"Herr Direktor Klett is away at a conference in Bern this week," she explained. "I am the Deputy Director, Ilse Sempel, at your service."

"We are making enquiries," Mason informed her, "regarding

a certain Dr. Seifert, who we understand used to be employed at this clinic."

"Heini?" asked the woman, in some surprise. "Is he somehow in trouble with the law?"

"He is, I regret to inform you, very much beyond the law."

Dr. Sempel's face fell.

"You mean he is no longer with us?" she asked, nervously.

"We are conducting an investigation into the circumstances of his death," Alison Aubrey explained. "Dr. Seifert's body was discovered in the town of Whalley, in northwest England, a few days ago. We are aiming to find out what we can of his background."

The Deputy Director gave a deep sigh and, fixing rather unbelieving eyes on the pair opposite her, said:

"Then you have come to the right place. Heini Seifert practiced medicine here for a number of years, prior to his retirement two years ago."

"In the field of…?" Mason asked.

"Organ transplants."

"Do you happen to know where he practiced before coming to Basel?"

"That was before my time," Ilse Sempel said. "But if I remember rightly, I think he came originally from Germany. From which area, I could not say."

"Did you also know his wife?" Alison asked.

"Celine? Why, of course. The couple both worked in Basel, here at this very clinic. She moved to Switzerland after a short spell in England to gain experience in the public sector. You know, the National Health Service is all very well for general purposes, and it does a very fine job for the most part. But if you want the very best, state-of-the-art treatments…."

"Yes, of course," George Mason interrupted, not wishing to hear a diatribe on public versus private medicine. "So the Seiferts were actually married right here in Basel?"

"And happily so, by all accounts, until Celine's untimely death."

The two detectives exchanged glances.

"Can you elaborate on that for us, Dr. Sempel?" Alison Aubrey asked.

"Celine died about twelve months before Heini retired. In fact, that event may have hastened his retirement, since he lived for his work."

"She died of natural causes?" Mason asked.

The Deputy Director nervously cleared her throat, rose from her chair and said, glancing hurriedly at her watch:

"I have a medical procedure to perform in a few minutes' time, if Scotland Yard will kindly excuse me. There was an inquest over Celine's death, followed by a trial, if you wish to look into it. That, too, was before I moved here from Geneva. The trial report will tell you much more than I ever could."

"Where would we obtain it?" Mason asked.

"The trial was widely covered by the local press at the time," Ilse Sempel informed him. "I suggest that you call at the offices of *Basler Zeitung* and consult the relevant newspaper editions on microfilm. If you are sufficiently conversant with the German language, that is." A questioning look accompanied her last remark, as if she entertained some doubts on that score.

Realizing that the brief interview was at an end, the detectives likewise rose and took their leave, thanking the woman for her valuable time.

"Is your German up to it, George?" Alison asked, the moment they stepped outside. "Dr. Sempel didn't seem to think it would be, if I read her rightly."

"They're a cagey lot, these medics," he replied. "I expect she could have told me a deal more than she did, as could the pharmacist. He too would have been fully conversant with the trial, but failed to make any reference to it, oddly enough. As for my German, I haven't used it much since that conspiracy I unearthed in Zurich some years back. I imagine I shall get the gist of things."

✦   ✦   ✦

Later that day, after resting a while and freshening up at their hotel, the Scotland Yard pair walked along the Rhine embankment until they came to a promising restaurant directly opposite Schifflande that served traditional Swiss fare. Since it was a fine evening, they opted to dine outdoors so that George Mason, who loved boats, could watch a large tourist vessel preparing to depart from the quay. He noted that it was only half-full, this early in the season. His young colleague, by contrast, closely studied the menu, trying to understand local cuisine as presented in German and French.

"You must help me out here, George," she said. "This menu's a complete mystery to me, even though I took some French at school."

The senior detective laughed sympathetically and willingly obliged.

"Raclettes is a typical dish from the French-speaking cantons," he explained. "It consists of cheese melted over potatoes and vegetables, served with pickles."

"I expect most Swiss dishes involve cheese, from the large dairy industry."

"We could try elsewhere and order steaks," he said.

"No, I should prefer something typically Swiss."

"Then how about Alplermagronen," her companion suggested. "Menus don't come more Swiss than that. Macaroni, Emmentaler cheese, onions, sun-dried tomatoes and strips of bacon. Served with apple sauce."

"Sounds most appetizing," Alison remarked.

George Mason appreciated her adventurousness, when most English visitors would probably opt for something familiar like roast beef or fish and chips. He regarded her fondly as she occupied herself with the wine list, noting the alert brown eyes beneath her dark, gamine-style hair.

"How's that fiancé of yours treating you?" he quipped, as soon as they had placed their order, to include a half-carafe of wine from the Valais, a region noted for its superior whites.

"Malcolm and I are doing just fine," she replied. "We have set our wedding date for early next year. You may even get an invitation."

"That I should be so honored!" he replied.

"Come off it, George," Alison said. "You know very well that you and Adele will be coming. But I am a bit unsure about asking Bill Harrington. What do you think?"

"The Chief Inspector? He's a grumpy old stick, to be sure, but I expect he would loosen up at a wedding reception. Especially after a few drinks. He's very partial to single-malt whiskey."

"I'll bear that in mind. Malcolm, as a Scot, is also something of a whiskey buff. He'll know what brands to stock. And, by the way, is Harrington married?"

"I believe so. But they lead very independent lives, both focused on their careers. It will help your prospects at the Yard if you include them. And they're sure to come up with a generous gift, reflecting their status."

"That's settled, then," Alison said, glad to have made that decision.

Their dinner arrived, commandeering their full attention. Within the restaurant, the resident pianist started playing what George Mason took to be a Brahms intermezzo, its dulcit strains wafting out across the patio overlooking the river, as the sun began to dip towards the Jura Mountains in the west, tingeing the city's pantile rooftops a deeper shade of red. He noted with approval that his young colleague ate with good appetite and seemed to be enjoying the hearty meal, typically eaten by alpine herdsmen. He admitted to himself that it was a good choice, even if he might have preferred, for the sake of his waistline, a lighter dish.

When they had done it full justice, they declined the waiter's offer of dessert, ordered coffee and absorbed the local atmosphere and the activity on the river. To George Mason, an evening like this was one of the main perks of a foreign assignment.

"Were you looking for wedding attire this afternoon?" he obliquely enquired.

The young sergeant was wrested from her reverie.

"You mean at the Marktplatz? Yes, I was, in a way. Thought I might pick up something suitable for a honeymoon trip. Or perhaps a dress for the end-of-term barbecue at Malcolm's school. He teaches economics."

"But you didn't find anything?"

"I didn't really have much time."

"Listen, Alison," he said, "there's not a lot of point in you accompanying me to the newspaper offices. I'll go over there first thing tomorrow morning and find out what I can about the trial. It'll take me a while to translate the German. I suggest you take the morning off to look round the stores and meet me around midday at Munsterplatz."

"That's very generous of you, George," Alison said, regarding him warmly. "I really would appreciate that. You really are sure you won't need me?"

"Not unless your German is better than mine."

Alison returned an ironic smile, which settled the matter. A half-hour later, they commenced strolling back to Hotel Balade in the encroaching dusk. Alison opted for a warm bath and an early night, while George Mason repaired to the lounge bar for a nightcap and a quiet hour reading the London *Times*.

◆　　◆　　◆

Leaving soon after breakfast the next day, to go their separate ways, they met up again at noon, as pre-arranged. Alison was carrying a bulky package under one arm as she breezed into the small café opposite the cathedral, where her colleague was waiting expectantly for her.

"I see you had some success," he remarked.

"Indeed I did," she replied. "Found just the thing for the school barbecue. A cotton print dress on sale at a department store downtown. I'll show it to you later. I would have paid nearly twice as much for it in London."

"Good for you," he replied. "I was waiting for you before ordering. Thought we'd have a light lunch to tide us over until dinner at the airport."

"Suits me," Alison said, quickly choosing a prawn open sandwich, while her companion opted for a half-pizza, with salad.

"I spent most of the morning at *Basler Zeitung*," he said. "A most interesting experience."

"Tell me all about it," she replied, all ears.

"It was quite a long trial, lasting more than two weeks. The state tried to establish that Heini Seifert murdered his wife."

"You don't say so!" Alison exclaimed.

"Celine apparently suffered from chronic back pain as the result of a skiing accident at Klosters. Her husband wrote the prescriptions for her medication, which were filled at Apotheke Ritter, surprise, surprise. Another explanation, probably, of the pharmacist's caginess yesterday, since he was called as a witness, by both the prosecution and the defense."

"You are saying that Dr. Seifert intentionally over-prescribed?"

"That's what the prosecution tried to claim. The drug used was acetominophen-based, which can prove fatal if the recommended dose is exceeded over a period of time."

"What was Seifert's defense?"

"That his wife had developed a tolerance for high dosages. He said that he was aware she sometimes exceeded the correct dose when the pain was particularly acute. But he also maintained that, as a trained nurse, she was conversant with the risks and knew what she was doing. In view of that, he did not see the need to monitor the situation too closely, which would have been impracticable anyway, given his busy schedule at the clinic."

"Sounds reasonable to me," Alison remarked.

"His lawyer," Mason continued, "offered two scenarios. One was that her death was accidental, the result of overdosing over a period of time; the other was that she had deliberately swallowed extra pills on the day she died."

"You mean that she took her own life?" a concerned Alison Aubrey asked. "What were the grounds for thinking that?"

George Mason drained the glass of Czech pilsner he had ordered while waiting for his colleague and cast his eye momentarily round the room, which was beginning to fill with tourists.

"Heini Seifert," he said, eventually, "claimed that his wife also suffered from periodic depression, because her back injury had left her less physically active. She was apparently a devotee of downhill skiing in winter and hiking in the Jura Mountains in summer. While she was not completely immobilized by her back problems – she continued with her nursing work, for example - her outdoor life was severely curtailed. She was also, he disclosed, a fairly heavy drinker."

"That all seems very plausible," Alison considered.

"An independent medical expert from the university was called as a witness for the defense. He testified that Celine Seifert's regular alcohol intake, combined with extra doses of acetaminophen over a period of time, would eventually have caused her death."

"That seems to rule out the suicide theory. So we're left with accidental death or murder."

"The jury, after being out for the best part of two days, returned a verdict of accidental death. One main reason for that, their foreman explained to the media, was that the prosecution had not provided a motive for murder. They had based their case on the fact that Dr. Seifert had written the prescriptions, and that he tolerated Celine's heavy drinking when, as her physician, he should have taken more control of the whole scenario."

"That's a very gray area," Alison conceded. "Seifert must have known full well that his wife was endangering her life, yet he did not intervene."

The waiter approached at that point, placing the light snacks before them. They ate in silence for a while, observing the other patrons of the café, whom Mason identified from snatches of overheard conversation as mainly French or German.

"Was there no evidence of marital problems?" the young sergeant asked, as they sipped lemon tea to round off their lunch.

"None whatsoever," her colleague replied. "The opposite seemed to be the case, as a matter of fact. The defense produced witnesses who testified to an, outwardly at least, harmonious relationship. This was particularly in evidence, according to testimony, at Klinik Mauser, where they both worked."

"So Heini Seifert walked free?"

"Indeed he did. He also retired a year later," Mason replied, glancing at his watch. "That could be around the time he moved to England. Now, at least, we have a clearer idea of his background."

"How much time do we have?" his companion asked.

"The airport bus leaves at four. That gives us an opportunity to look round the cathedral, since we are close by. It apparently contains the tomb of Erasmus."

"You're one up on me there, George," Alison said.

"A leading scholar and humanist of the Reformation era," he explained. "He stood for moderate reform of the church, rather than the clean break that eventually occurred under the Protestant leaders."

"You mean Martin Luther and his ilk?"

George Mason nodded.

"His Swiss counterpart," he continued, "was Ulrich Zwingli, who advocated a married clergy, among other progressive measures. He operated out of Zurich, but was killed in a pitched battle against Catholic loyalists from Luzern."

"They certainly took their religion seriously in those days," the younger officer mused.

"The so-called Wars of Religion lasted over a hundred years," Mason explained, "wreaking havoc over large areas of Europe."

"The upshot being," Alison remarked, "religious tolerance as we know it today."

"You know your history, too," he commented, approvingly. "Come, let us get a move on so we don't run out of time."

Chapter Three

Two days later, George Mason and Alison Aubrey arrived by train in Manchester around midday. The local police, by prior arrangement, offered them the use of an unmarked car to complete their journey north. They reached Whalley about an hour later, calling at the police station to speak with the officer-in-charge of this normally quiet, rural outpost. Sergeant Roy Wheeldon was expecting them.

"We've done a thorough check of this whole area," he informed them, "and have turned up nothing on an H. Seifert."

"His first name was Heini," Mason said. "We turned that up in Basel, where he used to work. He was a doctor of medicine."

"At least you have made some headway," Wheeldon remarked. "Unusual, don't you think, for a doctor to become a victim of murder?"

"This is an unusual case," came the reply. "One that's going to prove difficult to crack. Did you do the rounds of the local restaurants, as we suggested?"

"We did indeed," the sergeant replied. "There is a pub-restaurant called The Three Fishes on the back road to Stonyhurst College, about two miles from here, near a hamlet named Great Mytton. A waiter whom we interviewed there mentioned serving a gentleman approximately fitting the description we gave him of the victim, as to age, attire and general appearance. He served him lunch on the day before we found the body."

"Was he dining alone?" Alison Aubrey asked.

"No, he was accompanied by a younger man and by a much younger woman. The waiter recalled them quite readily, from the fact that he overheard them speaking in a foreign language."

"Would that be German, for example?" Mason asked.

"The waiter, an immigrant from Bangladesh, had no idea what language it was. He said simply that it did not sound like English. The waiter's own English, however, was halting. He is a fairly recent immigrant."

"That could be a significant development, Sergeant," the detective said, "if we could trace either of those two persons."

"I looked into that," the sergeant said, "hoping they had left a paper trail, in the form of a check or credit card receipt."

"But, of course, they paid in cash," Alison wryly remarked.

"Exactly," came the reply. "The Bangladeshi seemed to recall that it was the younger man who settled the bill."

Mason pondered that information for a moment.

"You have been most helpful, Sergeant," he complimented. "What you have told us may not have immediate significance, but it may help complete the picture at a later stage, depending on the progress of our enquiries."

The local officer, gratified to bathe in the high regard of Scotland Yard, offered them some freshly-brewed coffee, which they politely declined, explaining that they had matters to attend to in the city of Lancaster.

"Then I suggest you avoid the motorway, which is the long way round, but instead head for Whitewell and the Trough of Bowland. It is a quieter route and very scenic. The Queen herself owns large estates there, as part of the Duchy of Lancaster, quite often visiting her tenant farmers there. I've heard it said that it's her favorite part of England."

"You don't say so," an intrigued George Mason replied. "But I can well understand anyone growing fond of this part of the country."

"I second that sentiment," Alison Aubrey added.

"If you feel the need for refreshment on the way," Roy Wheeldon then said, "you could do a lot worse than call at Whitewell Inn, for a genuine country pub lunch."

"We may just do that," the detectives said, as they took their leave.

Less than an hour later, after a scenic drive through Bowland, which George Mason imagined took its name from medieval archery, they reached Lancaster. It was a medium-sized city dominated by the castle on a promontory overlooking the River Lune.

"It's from the same era as Whalley Abbey and last saw military action during the English Civil War," he explained to his young colleague. "Before Oliver Cromwell's time, it featured mainly in 14th Century conflicts with the Scots, who were prone to conducting raids across the border. Centuries before that, it was the site of a Roman camp."

"It certainly is an impressive structure," Alison replied, as they turned into the city's main street. "I'm not surprised they also used it as a prison."

"About as secure as prisons come, I should imagine," her colleague mused, pulling into a vacant parking space. "Not much chance of a midnight flit, judging by the heavy bars on the windows and the height of the walls."

Alison Aubrey smiled to herself at his turn of phrase, as Mason led the way inside the main post office to consult the area telephone book.

"Assuming that Celine Miller's parents are still alive," he said, "we should not have too much difficulty locating them."

"John and Betty Miller?" Alison enquired.

Mason nodded.

"No sign of them here, however," he remarked, after a few minutes. "Which could mean that they're ex-Directory."

"Or that they've moved to a different town."

"Also possible," George Mason agreed. "Only one way to find out. The City Hall is just a bit farther down the main street. We'll leave our car where it is, since we were lucky enough to find a parking spot, and go there on foot. If the Millers are still living in Lancaster, we should find their names on the property tax register."

With that, he led the way, at a brisk pace given his rather heavy build, to the municipal offices. A quick search of the rate-payers register, however, also proved fruitless.

"Rather odd, don't you think?" Alison Aubrey remarked, sensing his disappointment. "It must mean that they are no longer living here. Or that…"

Her voice trailed off at the implication.

"… they are no longer living," Mason added, matter-of-factly. "We can establish that at the Registry of Births and Deaths."

Returning to the main hall, they made enquiries at the information desk and were directed to an office on the second floor of the same building, reached by a wide wooden staircase. The duty clerk soon turned up the relevant records.

"Betty Miller died on November 17th, 2010," she said. "Her husband, John Miller, died the previous year, on August 30th, 2009. I can issue copies of the death certificates, if you so wish."

"That will not be necessary," George Mason replied. "But thanks, anyway. What might be helpful are records of their births." He was thinking that one or other of the Millers, if not both, might have been born in the Lancaster area.

The obliging clerk, on consulting the relevant records, shook her head.

"Neither of them was born in Lancaster," she informed them. "If you wish to learn their date and place of birth, you should enquire at Somerset House in London. They house all the regional records under one roof."

"We shall probably do that," Mason said, thanking her again as they turned to leave.

"That settles it," Alison said, as they retraced their steps back towards their car.

"What I propose now," her colleague said, "is a leisurely drive back through the Trough of Bowland, to see if we can't get ourselves a warm meal at Whitewell Inn. It's noted for local cuisine. Jugged hare, for example; or roast pheasant."

"Fine with me," the younger officer approvingly replied. "I love these out-of-the-way country pubs; they have such a unique and inviting atmosphere. I think I'll pass on the more exotic dishes, however. Something like brook trout, perhaps, or even another plowman's lunch. I really enjoyed what we had at Whalley."

"Suit yourself, Alison," Mason said. "They should have quite a broad menu. On the way back through Whalley, we'll call at The Three Fishes, to see if the Bangladeshi waiter can add anything to what he told Sergeant Wheeldon."

"That's good thinking."

"All being well, we shall be back in Manchester by early evening, and in London by nightfall. First thing tomorrow, go round to Somerset House and see what you can dig up on a John and Betty Miller. I have some loose ends to tie up on an earlier case at Swiss Cottage, which will take a little time."

+   +   +

Three days later, the Scotland Yard detectives were on their way to Dresden by an early-afternoon Lufthansa flight from Heathrow. Alison Aubrey had discovered, on her visit to Somerset House, that in 1991 John Miller had changed his name by deed poll from Johann Mueller. His wife Betty had done likewise, her original name being Beate Mueller. Further enquiries at Home Office

Immigration by the young detective, while George Mason was still tying up the Swiss Cottage case, had drawn the information that the Muellers had arrived in England from Germany earlier that same year.

"Didn't expect we'd be making another trip to Europe so soon," Mason remarked. "But if that's where the trail leads..."

He broke off mid-sentence as the air hostess appeared with trays of light refreshments including, Mason noted with approval, a small flask of Riesling.

"Heini Seifert's wife, Celine," his companion remarked, eyeing the offerings approvingly, "would presumably also be of German nationality."

"Which could mean," Mason said, "that Heini Seifert himself, if not of Swiss origin, was probably also a German national, as Ilse Sempel at Klinik Mauser intimated. We should be able to establish facts like that at the Stadthaus registry, first thing tomorrow morning."

"Interesting, don't you think, George, that the main pointers are now to Germany? You're an old hand at this sort of thing, but it's valuable experience for me, apart from affording a break from routine."

"I enjoy these European assignments," he replied. "You never really know what to expect, which gives them an extra dimension you don't get on home turf. What interests me right now is the visiting card retrieved from Seifert's jacket, which gives a Dresden address. That's as much as we have to go off for the time being. I'm banking on a possible connection between the Muellers and Heinrich Feldman."

"It may be a long shot," Alison considered. "Feldman and Seifert were both doctors, so their connection could have been a professional one. But where do Seifert's wife and her parents fit into the picture?"

"I am hoping that Dresden will throw some light on that. Chief Inspector Harrington is keen on quick results. He doesn't like spending police time on, quote, 'foreigners'. Not that he's particularly xenophobic; just that he thinks, and probably rightly, that we have enough home-grown problems to deal with."

"I take your point, George," Alison said. "He never struck me as notably broad-minded. I was rather surprised, in fact, when he agreed to hire a woman on his staff."

"That was more the Superintendent's doing, Alison. His wife's high up in legal circles, so he tends to promote gender equality, whenever possible; whereas Bill Harrington is more old-school."

With that, they settled into their light meal and relaxed for the remainder of the flight to Dresden, allowing Alison Aubrey to scan the pages of *Vogue*, while her colleague read the sports news in the London *Times*. Shortly after 5.00 p.m., their plane touched down at Klotzsche Airport, where they took the S-Bahn to Dresden Hauptbahnhof. On arrival, they took a taxi to the Holiday Inn in the Alstadt, the old quarter of the city, registered and freshened up in their first-floor rooms before setting out to explore their new environs. It was now just turned six and their thoughts turned to evening dinner. Threading their way through narrow streets lined with small shops and antique stores inviting their curious gaze, they passed several restaurants before entering the Britzer, an establishment specializing in German cuisine. The Altstadt, to George Mason's way of thinking, had a distinctly baroque atmosphere.

"Wasn't Dresden largely destroyed during the war?" Alison asked, as they took their seats in the far corner of the restaurant and perused the menu.

"Didn't you notice the charred buildings still very much in evidence on our way from the Hauptbahnhof?" her companion replied. "The city was fire-bombed in 1945. Around thirty thousand people are said to have lost their lives, and that figure is probably under-estimated."

"I suppose it was a form of tit-for-tat," Alison opined, "following the London blitz."

"There were, apparently, some valid strategic objectives too, apart from softening up the population. But I can't quite recall what they were. Immense damage was done to the historical heart of the city, which has since been restored to some of its former glory as capital of the Kingdom of Saxony."

"I've read about the rebuilding of the Frauenkirche, as a replica of the original church on that site."

"Britain donated the new cupola for it," Mason proudly observed, "as a form of reparation, or a gesture of goodwill. Take it how you will. The opera house, the Semper, is another example of successful restoration. We'll probably see both buildings during our stay here."

A young waitress in attractive regional costume approached their table, taking orders for a stein of local beer and a spritzer, respectively, before they chose items from the menu.

"Coventry Cathedral was also largely rebuilt after the war," Alison said. "Did Germany make a contribution to that?"

"I believe they did, in a way," Mason replied. "The Luftwaffe bombed it in 1940, as part of an operation called Moonlight Sonata, named after a Beethoven classic. I read somewhere that the nails retrieved from the ruins were formed into a cross that was solemnly consecrated in a Berlin cathedral."

"So there was forgiveness and reconciliation in the end, which is all to the good. I'll drink to that."

Momentarily somber, they raised and touched glasses.

"So what are we having for dinner tonight, George?" Alison asked, lightening the mood.

"I'll settle for the donner kebab, I think," Mason declared. "It says here that it's a German variation on a traditional Greek dish. Interesting to see what they come up with."

"Can you interpret this *Fische* menu for me?" she pleaded. "It's Greek to me."

"*Forelle gebacken* is baked trout," he replied, with a chuckle at her deft word-play. "And *Gefüllte Scholle* means stuffed plaice. The other items appear to be grilled cod, monkfish or swordfish."

"The plaice sounds fine to me," the young sergeant said, leaning back into her seat, pleased with her selection. "And, if you don't mind, George, I'll retire quite soon after we've eaten. I'm a bit tired after the journey."

"You can surely join me for a nightcap in the hotel bar," her colleague urged. "It will help you sleep."

"Perhaps," came the cautious reply, "For just a half-hour or so."

* * *

The following morning the two detectives, consulting a street-plan, made their way after breakfast through the narrow streets of the Altstadt, eventually arriving at the recently-built Stadthaus on Theaterstrasse. Following the same procedure they had used in Basel, they located the civil registry on the second floor of the building and asked the assistant to search the name Johann Mueller, to see if he was in fact a native of Dresden.

"It's not an uncommon name." the official informed them, peering at them over half-lenses. "Have you anything else to go off?"

"Only that his wife's name is Beate," George Mason said.

"Perhaps we had better start at the marriage register," came the rather terse reply.

With that, he disappeared into an adjoining office, leaving the two detectives in suspense for several minutes. When he returned, he produced a copy of the marriage certificate, which he obligingly translated for them.

"Reverend Johann Mueller and Beate Breuer were married on June 23rd, 1961," he explained, "at the Zionskirche in the Sudvorstadt area of the city. The parish was temporarily re-housed in an army barracks, following war damage to the original building."

"Herr Mueller was a clergyman, then?" Mason asked, in some surprise, inwardly pleased that his surmisal was proving correct.

"He was a minister of the Lutheran Evangelical Church."

"During the period, presumably, that Dresden was part of communist East Germany?"

"That is correct. But since 1990 we have thankfully – though not all Dresdeners would share that sentiment - been part of a united Germany."

"I read somewhere," Alison Aubrey put in, "that Protestant clergymen were very active later in the regime in promoting changes to the system."

"Particularly in Leipzig," came the reply. "But also here in our own historic city, even though on the whole relations between church and state were quite cordial."

"That was something I hadn't realized," Mason said. "Referring back to the Register of Births, do you have an entry for a Heinrich Feldman?"

The official's face registered surprise at yet more requests, but he complied nonetheless, shifting his focus to computerized records at the far side of the compact and well-organized office, whistling softly to himself what the detective took to be a Mozart aria. Within minutes, he had returned to the service counter.

"There is no one by that name in our records," he informed them.

George Mason felt a tinge of disappointment, but he did not show it.

"Do you have anything on a Heini Seifert?" he asked.

The official returned a look of veiled hostility, as a small queue was beginning to build behind the two visitors.

"If you have a list of names," he snapped, "it will save me both time and legwork if you let me have them all at once."

"I beg your pardon," Mason said, "for imposing on your good offices like this. Heini Seifert is, in fact, the last person my colleague and I are trying to trace, and we are deeply grateful for your assistance."

The official seemed mollified at that remark, glancing with approval at the attractive young woman accompanying the rather portly Englishman. He re-crossed the room at a brisker pace, consulted the records and again returned a negative.

"Does that conclude your business?" he asked. "There are other people waiting."

"It does indeed. May I take this copy of the marriage certificate?"

"For a fee of two euros."

George Mason fished in his pocket for two coins, handed them over and thanked the man again before leading the way back down to street-level, where he consulted his map and headed down towards the embankment of the River Elbe.

"Interesting, don't you think," his colleague said, "that Johann Mueller was a reverend?"

"Especially so, Alison, since he was not recorded as such in the Lancaster registry."

"Which could mean that he gave up the ministry on arrival in England."

"For reasons yet to be discovered," Mason added.

"But we still have no records of either Feldman or Seifert," Alison complained.

"So our next move," he replied, "will be to pay a visit to Ufergasse 219B which, according to this street-plan, we should be able to locate by following the river eastwards."

A few minutes' walk took them to the grassy purlieus of the embankment, where natives of Dresden were taking moderate exercise in the morning air, strolling, playing ball games or simply reading books and newspapers. Others were priming grills for a midday barbecue. It was a relaxed, carefree atmosphere, well-suited to this city of high culture and tourism, belying the devastation it had suffered during the war. They paused for a few moments to watch a large paddle-steamer approach the quay, its giant wheels slowing almost to a standstill as they noisily churned the water. Tourists crowding the foredeck waved to friends, relatives and even to complete strangers ashore.

Following the course of the river for several minutes, the two detectives soon struck Ufergasse, a narrow tree-lined alley leading from the embankment to the main thoroughfare of Neue Strasse. George Mason soon located No. 219B, pulled the old-fashioned metal handle of the doorbell, which gave a noisy ring, and waited. There was no reply. He stepped back and glanced up at the curtained windows of the three-storey terraced building, but saw no one. He rang again, noticing a lace curtain pull slightly back at ground-floor level. Moments later, he heard bolts being drawn back on the inside. An elderly man with a wispy white beard slowly opened it and peered out.

"*Was wollen Sie?*" he asked, suspiciously.

"We are detectives from England," George Mason said, "pursuing enquiries regarding a gentleman named Heinrich Feldman, whom we believe was a medical practitioner."

"*Polizei!*" exclaimed the concierge, taken aback.

"May we come inside for a few moments?" Alison Aubrey asked.

"If you must," the man replied, leading the way through a door to the left of the hallway. It opened on a small office, beyond which comfortable living quarters were visible. He bade them take a seat, before crossing to the living-room to switch off the television. When he returned, he sat opposite them on a high-backed antique chair.

"We believe Dr. Feldman used this address," Mason began.

"Yes, that is so. But it is already some years ago," came the astonished reply. "I have lost all contact with him and could not even be sure he is still living in this city."

"Can you tell us what you know about him?" Alison asked.

"Dr. Feldman was a good tenant," the concierge informed them. "He always paid his rent on time. He was regular in his habits and did not cause any problems. Unlike some of the other tenants, I might add."

"What was his specialism as a doctor?" Mason asked.

"He was more than a doctor, he was a well-known surgeon. At one of our main hospitals, but I forget which one. Top medical personnel tend to move on to higher things. They don't stay long in one post."

"Married or single?" Alison asked.

"Divorced," the other said. "He moved in here soon after the decree came through, claiming that he was too busy at the hospital to maintain a large residence. This place seemed to suit him admirably. He often remarked on how peaceful and relaxing the neighborhood was. He took his meals at local restaurants, since our apartments have only rudimentary cooking facilities – enough to make warm drinks and snacks."

"What were his main activities after work, as far as you were aware?" George Mason asked.

"He was very active in politics, I do know that. He also took an interest in the cultural life of the city, particularly in chamber music. Apart from that, he was a keen skier who went regularly to Garmisch in the Bavarian alps."

"When you say politically active, do you mean that he stood for government office?" Alison asked.

The concierge gave a hollow laugh.

"In the old days," he replied, "under the Communist regime, there were no such things as free elections."

"You mean," Mason interposed, "that the Communist Party drew up the list of candidates and you could not vote for alternatives?"

"Precisely so," the concierge replied, "except that it was called the Socialist Unity Party. Its monopoly on power was effectively backed by the Stasi."

"The Secret Police?" a pensive Alison enquired.

The man gravely nodded.

"They pervaded every area of civil life," he said, "keeping thousands of files on all manner of people. They even encouraged us to inform on members of our own families, to keep tight control over what they considered subversive elements, fledgling opposition movements, capitalist lackeys and so forth. It was a difficult time. Families were often divided against themselves."

"I can well believe that, Herr…?" Mason commiserated, feeling himself warming to his candid interlocutor, who obviously had no regrets at the passing of the old order.

"….Grass. Dieter Grass, at your service. Excuse my alarm when you said you were from the police – it revived old memories, best forgotten."

"How did Dr. Feldman fit into this general picture?" Alison Aubrey asked.

"I should say that he worked in close cooperation with the authorities," Grass replied. "As an employee of the state – as were all medical personnel in those days – he would be expected to demonstrate his loyalty from time to time, to maintain his position."

Having said that, he abruptly stood and withdrew to a back room, leaving his visitors to ponder his exact meaning. Within minutes, he returned with a large tray bearing a pot of tea, crockery and slices of fruit cake.

"I am aware," he said, with a sly smile as he set the tray down before them, "that, being from England, you will not refuse a cup of tea."

The surprised visitors laughed heartily at that remark, watching with interest as the concierge deftly completed this most English of rituals using his best china, correctly adding the milk first. They partook of the welcome refreshment in silence for a few minutes, as the siren of a police car penetrated the house. George Mason took advantage of the hiatus to glance round the room. On the dresser was a photograph of a much younger Dieter Grass in military uniform. Probably a form of mandatory military service, he mused, since the subject was too young to have seen action in the war. Opposite it was a later likeness showing him in linked arms with a tall blonde. His wife, the detective wondered? But he did not enquire, out of tact. Nudging his plate aside, he said:

"Are you implying that Heinrich Feldman also acted as an informer?"

Dieter Grass swallowed his last morsel of fruit cake, which he evidently relished, cleared his throat and said:

"There was a high-profile case, in 1986 or thereabouts, in which a prominent theologian named Johann Mueller was put on trial for subversion. Dr. Feldman was a leading witness at the trial, which resulted in a stiff prison term for the minister."

The Scotland Yard pair exchanged glances at the mention of Reverend Mueller, but did not disclose the nature of their interest in him.

"That is most interesting, Herr Grass," Mason remarked. "Was there a family connection?"

"Not that I know of," came the reply. "Dr. Feldman did in fact re-marry, but I never met his new bride. He did mention something about a honeymoon in Tuscany, but that is about all I recall on that subject. I do not even remember her name after all these years."

"Where could we acquire information on Mueller's trial?" George Mason asked.

"Go to the Stadthaus," the concierge said. "The Stasi's secret files, many thousands of them, were opened to public inspection soon after reunification."

"We shall likely do that," Mason said, as the two detectives rose to take their leave. "One more thing. Did you ever meet a Heini Seifert?"

"How would I have done?" Dieter Grass challenged.

"We are assuming he was a medical colleague of Feldman's," Alison Aubrey told him. "Perhaps also from Dresden."

The concierge accompanied them through the hallway and out the front door.

"Dr. Feldman was not from Dresden," he said. "I had the impression, from his accent, that he came from the north. From Hamburg, perhaps, or Bremen. As to the possible medical associate you indicated, a person I have never met, I should mention that Heini is Swiss rather than German. A diminutive form of Heinrich. Does that answer all your questions?"

"For the time being, certainly," George Mason said. "Thank you very much for your time and for the refreshment. Genoa cake is one of my favorites."

"You are most welcome," Grass replied, shutting the street door behind them.

◆   ◆   ◆

"Heini Seifert and Heinrich Feldman are two very elusive characters," Alison Aubrey remarked, as they neared the end of their brief lunch break at an outdoor restaurant fronting the Elbe.

"I am certainly not about to go searching for their origins in northern Germany," her colleague tartly replied, watching with interest a paddle-steamer preparing to leave the quay. "At least, from the talkative Herr Grass we might have made a useful connection."

"Between Feldman and Mueller? I agree that looks promising. Do you think, George, that might explain Reverend Mueller's move to England?"

"On the assumption that he was freed from prison soon after reunification of East and West Germany," Mason considered, "he may well have been looking for a fresh start in life, to put that unfortunate episode behind him."

"Whilst also giving up the ministry," his young colleague said.

"A completely fresh start, in that case."

"This business doesn't put Feldman in a very good light, does it?"

"As a Stasi informer?" Mason asked. "Too early to judge, until we can get more facts. Finish your drink, Alison and we'll spend part of the afternoon going through the files of the former secret police. They should prove interesting reading!"

When they reached the Stadthaus twenty minutes later, the senior archivist was helpful to the point of offering a translation service. George Mason demurred, confident that he could handle the language well enough to get the general sense. He did not want a verbatim report of the proceedings. They took the heavy dossier, retrieved from a long bank of filing cabinets, to a spare desk, opened it and perused the contents, the detective sergeant poised to take notes. It did not take George Mason very long to ascertain the main charges against Reverend Johann Mueller. There were two of them, backed up by copious documentation including statements from witnesses. The first, and more serious charge, was that Mueller had helped people flee into West Germany.

"It was done," he explained in a low voice to Alison, "if my understanding of all this is correct, by organizing pastoral visits to the West, through Magdeburg and across the border. A minibus carrying parishioners from the Dresden area would attend, say, a conference or retreat in West Germany, but the number on the return trip would be one or two individuals less than on the outward journey. This practice continued for a period of years, helping quite a fair number of East Germans to escape."

"But surely the border guards would have checked the manifest in both directions and discovered a discrepancy?" Alison protested.

"It says here," her colleague continued, "that numbers were indeed carefully checked on the first few occasions. Afterwards, the guards grew laxer, doing a head count only on the outward trip and cheerily waving them back through on their return. Because they were a church group, they were apparently considered trustworthy and above suspicion. Johann Mueller was able to exploit that trust."

"How daring and clever of the Reverend," an impressed Alison remarked. "But how did the authorities eventually tumble to the deception?"

George Mason grimaced.

"Get this, Alison," he replied. "No less a person than Dr. Heinrich Feldman took part in one such exchange, as consultant to a program to send medical missionaries to East Africa. He is recorded here, with a commendation for loyalty to the state."

"And what was the second charge against Mueller?"

"That he was a member of an underground opposition party," Mason replied. "According to his statements at the trial, the Reverend denied that he had any interest in politics, claiming that his work was purely pastoral."

"The party in power, the Socialist Unity Party that Dieter Grass mentioned, did not permit any challenge to its monopoly, then?" Alison asked.

"In theory, no," Mason explained. "But reading between the lines, it seems that other political parties did exist, but did not attract sufficient support to be considered a threat. For that reason they were tolerated, if frowned upon. Reverend Mueller claimed only that his rectory was used for meetings by such a group, but that he did not take part in their proceedings."

"Guilt by association?"

"Something on those lines. But taken together with the previous charge, it did not improve his standing with the court."

George Mason read further, while Alison took brief notes. After a few moments, he said:

"Apparently, Johann Mueller had already served a prior prison term in his youth, presumably some time before his ordination. It is noted here as part of his general record, with the date of his release."

"What on earth for?" his young colleague asked.

Mason re-scanned the complex German, to make sure he had got things right.

"It seems he took part in an anti-Communist uprising in 1953 which was suppressed by the patriotic state police with the help of Soviet forces. I imagine that was quite a shindy, much like the Czech uprising in 1968."

"Didn't Russian tanks move into Wenceslas Square in Prague, causing the collapse of the government on account of its liberalizing policies?"

"Indeed they did," he replied, with an appreciative smile at her political acumen. "It took another thirty years for the East European regimes to collapse, and I believe the Lutheran Church played a key role in promoting reform. Go ask the archivist about church-state relations during that period, just to fill out the picture, while I finish this file."

Alison Aubrey gladly accepted the assignment, spending fully fifteen minutes speaking with the helpful official. When she returned to their desk, her colleague was getting ready to leave, feeling the need for fresh air after his mental exertion, requesting that she reserve any new information for later on. His head was fairly spinning already. They commenced walking back to their hotel, pausing now and then to look at shop window displays, mainly of apparel, that appealed to the young sergeant. Mason considered they had quite a bit of new material to absorb. He would like to mull it over alone for a while and rest a little before freshening up for dinner. Alison thought she would take a deep bath, to relax her limbs after all the legwork. George Mason, she knew, was a great one for exploring foreign cities on foot, when the likes of Bill Harrington would have used taxis.

It was just turned six o'clock when, much refreshed, the two detectives re-emerged from the Holiday Inn into the cool evening sunshine. They explored the narrow streets of the Altstadt for a while, enjoying the performances of street musicians Dresden was noted for. Among the violinists, cellists, saxophonists and the like, they came across a young man playing classical music on a grand piano set back in a pedestrianized area. He attracted a mixed group of listeners, including two British detectives, for his adroit rendering of a Beethoven sonata. Alison Aubrey, in particular, was completely charmed, never before having witnessed such activities;

whereas cosmopolitan George Mason had seen similar in Zurich, but never a grand piano.

Continuing their exploration of the old quarter, they eventually found a restaurant serving traditional German dishes. Entering, they were shown to a table in the corner of a room decorated Saxon style, presumably to complement the cuisine. The waitress, in regional costume, greeted them warmly, presenting a menu and wine list. George Mason scanned them both, reading items of interest to his companion.

"They do eat a lot of pork here, don't they?" Alison remarked, having already learned the word *Schwein*.

"It's their favorite food," Mason replied. "They enjoy heavy meals, generally of meat, potatoes and vegetables."

"They like their sausages, too," the young sergeant said, having also picked up the word *Wurst*, "in almost endless variety. But what about fish?"

"You could have *Scholle gebacken*," he explained. "Baked plaice, in plain English."

"Sounds good. So what will you have, George?"

"I'm opting for Bavarian bratwurst, with sauerkraut," he replied. "As for wine, I recommend we try an Ahr Valley red. Germany is known mainly for its white wines, but the region near the Eiffel Mountains produces very palatable reds."

"You're so *au fait*, George," an impressed Alison said. "And where exactly is the River Ahr?"

"In the northwest," came the quick reply. "The Ahr is a tributary of the Rhine, flowing due east from near the Belgian border and the Ardennes."

"Isn't that where the Battle of the Bulge took place?"

"It certainly was," Mason confirmed. "So called because the Germany Army mounted a surprise attack late in the war, causing a huge dent in Allied defenses, dubbed 'the Bulge'. General Patton and the US Third Army played a key role in the counter-offensive and ultimate rout of the enemy."

"With lots of casualties, I suppose?" Alison said.

"Tens of thousands wounded or killed, on both sides," came the reply. "It was the heaviest action American forces saw in World War 11."

That said, they turned their attention to more urbane matters, placed their order for food and relaxed to the sound of hurdy-gurdy music from the street outside, as the tables around them started to fill with patrons, including foreign visitors like themselves. George Mason, adept at languages, overheard snatches of French, Swiss-German and Dutch.

"So what did the archivist at the Stadthaus have to say earlier, regarding church-state relations?" he began, having tasted the wine and watched the waitress pour two full measures.

"He was most informative," Alison said. "I think he enjoyed dishing the dirt on the Communist regime."

"I can imagine."

"He told me that the East German government began to promote what it called 'scientific atheism'. The Lutheran Church grew alarmed at the drainage of members, especially of the young, who might have consid ed their career prospects limited by church-going. At first hostile to the socialist regime, church leaders decided to accept its legitimacy and cooperate with it, in order to influence affairs from within the system, rather than remain outsiders. That marked a turning point. The state, for its part, grew less hostile to the Church, arriving at a sort of modus vivendi with it. For example, they allowed clerical personnel certain privileges, one of which was foreign travel to ecumenical conferences and the like. And they did not interfere in the internal affairs of the church, such as in the appointment of bishops and recruitment to seminaries."

"Which would explain how Reverend Mueller got to travel to the West," Mason considered. "I must admit that it puzzled me at first that he was allowed to come and go so freely, given the typical restrictions in place for the mass of East German citizens."

"Until Heinrich Feldman came on the scene," Alison said.

"What was his precise relationship to Heini Seifert? That is something I should very much like to discover."

"A professional connection, from the looks of it," Alison Aubrey thought. "Perhaps nothing more than that."

"I have a sneaking suspicion there may well be more to it," Mason said, as they turned their attention to the appetizing meal set before them.

"The archivist also told me some chilling facts about Stasi interrogation methods," Alison said after a while, between forkfuls of plaice.

"And?" her interested colleague enquired.

"He said that they employed non-stop questioning, as an effective technique. An innocent suspect, they figured, would grow increasingly distressed, even hysterical, as the interrogation continued. A guilty person, on the other hand, would remain relatively calm and calculating, aware that he had something to hide, at all costs."

George Mason's eyes narrowed, as he finished chewing a piece of spicy Bavarian sausage.

"How cynical is that," he remarked. "They must have been briefed by professional psychologists to come up with techniques like that."

"He also told me that there were over two hundred thousand informers in East Germany, at any one time."

Mason swallowed hard.

"Aren't you glad, Alison," he said, "that we don't live in a police state?"

Chapter Four

Marika Grigorev relaxed on a recliner on the window balcony of her hotel room. Rydal Hall, in Bowness-on-Windermere, was a five-star establishment she had come to regard almost as a second home after her arrival in England two years ago. Two or three times a year, when business was slack, usually in the spring and late-autumn, she would book in for a few days. She raised herself on one arm to grasp the jug of fresh coffee room service had just delivered, poured a cup and nibbled at the remains of the croissants left over from the breakfast. She then lit a cigarette to enjoy with the coffee and directed her gaze out over the extensive, wooded grounds of the hotel to Lake Windermere beyond, its vast expanse of water glinting in the strong sunshine. She watched the vintage motor launch, the *Teal*, draw alongside the jetty to take on waiting passengers for the trip to Ambleside, thinking that she too, since it was such a fine day, might sample the afternoon voyage.

Glancing round at her upscale surroundings, she congratulated herself on the remarkable turn-around in her personal circumstances. A few years ago, she had been a trainee nurse struggling to make an adequate living in a modern suburb of Bucharest.

The newly-built private hospital which initially hired her had suddenly closed its doors after being hit by the mortgage-loan crisis, leaving her high-and-dry with the final stage of her internship uncompleted. State hospitals were also affected, so there seemed to be little prospect of her acquiring the coveted qualification of registered nurse. By one of those strange twists of fate she was unable to explain, she had met her future husband Ivo a few weeks later, at a night club in downtown Bucharest, where she had obtained evening work as a waitress. He spent liberally, on himself and on the group of friends who sometimes accompanied him, and that had made a deep impression on a hard-up former student. No matter that he was about twenty years her senior, she had had no reservations about accepting a dinner date, which led to more dates and to a marriage proposal.

She recalled, as sparrows alighted on her balcony to peck at breakfast crumbs, her surprise when Ivo had informed her that he was back in Bucharest on vacation from Rotterdam. Without going into precise details, he gave the impression of being in some sort of specialized medical field, and that he could help her gain experience that might eventually count towards her elusive qualification. All of this had been music to her ears. She had, naturally, a few initial qualms about leaving her home turf and her family, but none at all about giving up her night club job and setting her sights on Western Europe, long the Mecca of citizens of the former Iron Curtain countries, whose economies were striving to match those of the West. She had spent only a few months in Holland, however, before Ivo booked passages on the overnight ferry from Hook of Holland to Hull, a major port on England's northeast coast. Ivo retained his luxury apartment in an upscale area of Rotterdam, dividing his time between the two European Union countries; while she herself was to be permanently stationed in England. English life and customs, its undulating countryside and the friendly reserve of its people had captivated her from the outset.

Rising at length from the recliner, with the feeling of having done justice to the full English breakfast, she attempted once more to contact Dr. Seifert on his cell phone, before taking a warm shower and dressing for a brief shopping trip to Bowness. She had tried to ring him several times the previous day, but without success. It puzzled her. She was aware that he had left his clinic for a few days on what he had described as personal business, whatever that meant. And not knowing anything at all about his family affairs – he was such a close individual – she had no idea of his current whereabouts. It nagged at her a little, as she passed through the French windows into her well-appointed bedroom, slipped off her designer night clothes and entered the shower. She needed to inform the surgeon that Ivo was arriving the next day with a new client from Holland.

◆　　◆　　◆

That same morning, Ivo Grigorev rose early in his luxury apartment in an upscale area of Rotterdam, one that had been largely spared the devastation of Nazi bombing in World War 11, preserving much of its original character and ambience. Disinclined in the absence of his wife to prepare his own meals, he dressed unhurriedly and strolled across the street to a neighborhood café, where he ordered a light breakfast of coffee and croissants. On fine mornings like this, he liked to sit at an outdoor table on the patio beneath chestnut trees just coming into leaf, so that he could also indulge in one of his favorite Dutch cigars. He felt at peace with the world, having telephoned Marika the previous evening to assure himself that all was well with her, feeling little concern at her difficulty in contacting Dr. Seifert. To his mind, there was probably a quite simple and straightforward explanation.

As he sipped his coffee and lit his cigar, he reflected with satisfaction on the fortuitous circumstance of his meeting with Heini Seifert. The doctor had advertised in a leading Dutch newspaper,

De Telegraf, for a medically-qualified assistant. A written reply to a box number had led to an early meeting, which hardly resembled a formal interview since it took place over drinks in a downtown pub. The two men struck an immediate rapport. Ivo outlined his qualifications in general medicine, while confessing that he had been struck from the Bucharest medical register for unethical conduct. A more amused than shocked Dr. Seifert asked him to expand on that. When he learned that it concerned a female patient, he had brushed the matter aside without more ado. That sort of thing, he had told Grigorev, was an occupational hazard of medical practice, and one could not always be sure where the truth of the matter lay. Some doctors and dentists did notoriously take advantage of female patients; some women, for reasons best known to themselves, were not above making false accusations.

It was almost mid-morning when a slim, tanned individual dressed in a dark-gray suit and sporting sunglasses approached his table, sat down and immediately ordered a latte. Ivo Grigorev had been expecting him, having met him on numerous previous occasions at this same spot over the course of the past two years.

"All is arranged," the newcomer said, dispensing with small talk.

"His name?" Ivo enquired.

"Zivko Plesijc. I have had a passport and papers made out for him by our usual expert in Amsterdam. Plesijc will be expecting you outside Delft train station at 2 p.m. He will recognize you by the dark-blue sailor's cap you normally wear for these contacts, plus the cigar you will light immediately on leaving the station concourse."

Having said as much, he handed over a sealed Manilla envelope.

"Everything you need is in there," he added, "passport, ID and two tickets for the overnight ferry from Hook of Holland to Hull. All you have to provide are the necessary train fares at either end of the journey."

"Your customary efficiency," Ivo remarked.

"It's what I am paid to do," the other blandly remarked, as he savored the fresh coffee and lit a cigarette.

Ivo gazed at the other man, he knew only as Fedor, in some admiration. It was no easy matter getting economic migrants into the United Kingdom. They could travel from one end of Europe to the other without passport controls, as a result of the Schengen Treaty that many European countries had signed up to. Britain, because it was such a big draw for migrants both legal and illegal, had opted out of that arrangement and was not included in the so-called Schengen Area. Careful and detailed preparations had therefore to be made to get people through UK Customs, whose officers manned each port of entry. Fedor's manner relaxed markedly as he sipped his coffee. He made a few general remarks about the network, supply lines and possible future concerns, before wishing Ivo Grigorev a pleasant and problem-free trip. He then drained his cup, stubbed out his cigarette, abruptly rose and proceeded to his car parked a short distance down the street.

Ivo left soon afterwards, calling at the city branch of his bank before continuing his way on foot to Rotterdam Centraal, where he caught the next train to Delft, noted for its fine pottery. On the way, he reflected on the success of Heini Seifert's business plan. The doctor had opened a clinic just outside the market town of Clitheroe, with the ostensible purpose of performing vasectomies and other procedures relating to male reproductive health. It formed the perfect cover for the more profitable side of the business, which was to perform kidney transplants for wealthy clients. The organ recipients paid sixty thousand pounds for the privilege. The donors, on the other hand, were allowed illegal entry into Britain and given one thousand pounds to help with living expenses before obtaining employment in the black economy, by firms eager to hire them off their books for low wages, so that they did not have to pay social insurance costs. The donors eventually wound up in the larger industrial cities, such as Leeds, Manchester and Birmingham, quickly disappearing into the general population.

Ivo Grigorev occasionally pondered the ethics of this operation, salving his conscience with the notion that the donors, even though callously exploited, had achieved their ambition to reach English shores and take advantage of its generous welfare services, including free health care. So they were invariably thankful and raised no difficulties, remaining unaware of the market value of their traded organ. His qualms were further assuaged by the fact that he himself received fifteen per cent of the overall fee, for what he regarded as the trickiest part of the operation. The donors were obtained through the extensive Omega Network, whose cut was thirty-five per cent. It was a large organization specializing in various forms of human trafficking, including vital organs, prostitution and economic migration for those able to afford the high up-front fee. Its tentacles reached as far east as Turkey, with a major emphasis on East Europe, particularly Albania, Kosovo, and Romania. The balance of the transaction went to Dr. Seifert, who paid Marika a salary for nursing and administrative services, financed his clinic and banked the rest. The arrangement suited Ivo very well, in that he could spend most of each month assisting in the day-to-day routine activities of the clinic, which he was well-qualified to do, and in living the high life with his young wife, Marika. One organ donor per month, albeit with attendant risks, substantially raised their income profile.

Zivko Plesijc spotted him the moment he emerged from Delft station. He was a youngish man who gave the impression of having seen the rougher side of life. Although in no way unkempt, being clean-shaven and of generally tidy aspect, his clothes were well-worn and his shoes down-at-heel. After brief mutual introductions in Serbo-Croat – Zivko spoke no English and Ivo had a smattering of the main East European tongues – they caught a bus just about to leave for Hook of Holland. Two hours later, they were on the high seas courtesy of North Sea Ferries. Zivko, who came originally from Belgrade, had never seen the ocean, spending the interval before dinner roaming the decks to take it all in, marveling at the sea birds and the varieties of small and large craft. Ivo Grigorev, for whom the sea was just a gray, amorphous mass, was content to occupy a stool in the forward bar. Only once, in all the crossings he had made to England and back, had the sea been rough, with mountainous waves that caused the boat to pitch so violently that the smorgasbord comestibles had washed all over the dining-room floor. Even members of the crew had been sea-sick.

Later on, over a dinner of grilled halibut, baked potatoes and a half-carafe of Muscadet, he drew his companion more out of his shell. He liked to establish a relationship of sorts with his 'clients', partly to put them at ease about what lay ahead, partly to reassure himself that the subject would not pose problems at a later stage. To that end, he was wont to show them a letter, printed on Ministry of Health stationery and signed by a civil servant, certifying the Clitheroe clinic and validating the procedures performed there. It invariably made the desired impression.

"Dr. Seifert is one of the leading specialists in his field," he said. "After a couple of days to rest and recover, you will be up and about again, starting a new life."

"It is all a little intimidating," the young man replied, visibly relieved as Grigorev translated the ministry letter for him.

"You must be very keen to get to England," Ivo said.

"I am looking forward to it," came the assured reply. "My girlfriend Anna moved there last fall, to take up a nursing job at a hospital in Manchester. I have tried all legal means to rejoin her, but without success. Serbia is not a member of the European Union; otherwise, I would have had no problem moving to Britain."

"Perhaps Serbia will join in due course," Ivo Grigorev observed.

"That may take years," Zivko replied. "I cannot wait that long. To me, this deal is worth it. I know of several people who live full lives with only one kidney."

His companion felt pangs of conscience at hearing that, suppressing it with the thought that his latest victim at least seemed to have no misgivings, and that he had someone who would welcome him after leaving the clinic. But there were possible snags in that, he reflected uneasily. A nurse, especially, would know the workings of the British health-care system and might mention Zivko's operation in official quarters. Or she might make a loose remark in the hearing of a medical colleague, who would report it to the authorities. The die was now cast, however, and there was no turning back. Omega should have uncovered such a relationship, had they done their homework. In the unlikely prospect of problems down the road, he and Marika would beat a quick retreat to Bucharest, leaving Seifert to hold the can. His loyalty to the doctor was based solely on monetary considerations.

"Tell me, Zivko," he said, regaining his buoyancy, "in Belgrade, do they still have that point-duty policeman who directs traffic with an elaborate ballet routine?"

The Serb broke into a huge smile, that his companion should be aware of something so typical of his native city.

"I think he retired some years ago," he replied. "I admit he gave a great performance daily at one of our key traffic intersections, drawing large crowds of onlookers. In fact, he was one of our main tourist attractions."

"You will find nothing like that in England," Ivo assured him. "The British are far too reserved in their demeanor."

"But they are... friendly people...yes?" Zivko enquired, hesitantly.

"Absolutely. They tend to socialize most evenings, after work, in the local pub."

"What is pub?"

"A public house, where they serve beer, spirits and light meals," Ivo explained. "They have music, too, either live or wired. And they play games such as darts, cards and dominoes. Very sociable. You will love it. Take your friend Anna for an evening out, when you meet up with her."

"Sounds good," Zivko said, warming to the idea.

"You will need money," Ivo cautioned. "We have a contact in Manchester who runs a chain of filling stations. He will most likely offer you a job, to help you get established and find your feet."

"That is very kind of you," the young man said, impressed at how comprehensive was the deal he had entered into.

They concluded their meal on friendly terms, just as Ivo Grigorev had planned. He congratulated himself on having won the young man's confidence, as they left the dining-room to stroll the upper deck in the fresh sea air and smoke Dutch half-coronas. An hour later, as the moonless night closed in, enveloping the sea in darkness save for the lights on a distant ship, they withdrew to the lower deck. The private cabins being booked up, to Ivo's annoyance, they joined other passengers in the main lounge, occupying reclining seats for an indifferent night's sleep. But not before Ivo had bought cans of Boddington's beer, to give his young charge a foretaste of English pub life while they watched the last half of a gangster movie on television.

The North Sea ferry docked at Hull early the following morning, after a smooth passage. Ivo Grigorev and Zivko Plesijc made their way after debarkation to the train station, where they awaited the next express to Leeds, taking advantage of an interval of twenty minutes to buy coffee and rolls at the station buffet. Mention of Leeds intrigued the young Serb, recognizing it as the home of a Premier League soccer club. Like many Europeans, he took a keen interest in English football, which was an additional reason for his wish to settle in Britain. On reaching the Yorkshire city late-morning, they changed platforms for the local train to Clitheroe, arriving at Wellman Clinic by taxi just after midday. Marika rushed out to greet them.

"I'm so relieved that you've got back safely," she said, her voice betraying anxiety.

"Is there a problem?" her husband immediately asked.

"Dr. Seifert," she replied. "He was due back here two days ago, but there has been no word from him. I have tried many times to reach him by cell phone, without success."

Ivo Grigorev stopped in his tracks, placing his valise on the ground as Serb, sensing something was wrong, looked on in puzzlement. Ivo seemed to be weighing the implications of her surprise announcement, while Marika simply stood there, at a loss.

"Let's not just stand here," she said, recovering her poise. "Come inside. I have prepared a nice lunch for you both."

The two travelers followed her in through the front door of the building and into a small kitchen at the rear. She bade them sit at a table covered with a checkered cloth, on which were placed cold cuts, mixed salad and freshly-baked bread. The men were hungry after their long train journey and fell to with keen appetites, while the weight-conscious Marika merely nibbled at the food.

"There must be some plausible explanation," Ivo eventually remarked. "Perhaps he has simply been delayed by family matters."

"That is what I have been telling myself," his wife rejoined. "But I still cannot understand why I have been unable to contact him."

Ivo Grigorev shrugged, stirring a spoonful of sugar into a cup of hot tea.

"We shall have to wait a few more days and see," he said. "I shall continue with the routine work of the clinic for the time being. There are two vasectomies, I believe, scheduled this week."

"And a client with erectile dysfunction," Marika added. "He booked an appointment only yesterday."

Having said that, she glanced in Zivko's direction. Ivo caught the implication. If Dr. Seifert did not show up, that would place the young Serb in an awkward position. It would also cause problems for the organ recipient.

"When is Seifert's next operation scheduled for?" he asked.

"Tomorrow morning, at 9.30."

"Then you must contact the client and inform him that the operation has to be postponed until further notice."

"What reason do I give?" his wife asked, nervously.

"That the surgeon, with regrets, is currently indisposed."

"And if Seifert does not return to Clitheroe, for whatever reason, what do we do then?"

Ivo pondered that for a few moments, while sipping his tea and drawing on a cigarette. Zivko rounded off his meal with a generous portion of Yorkshire pudding, freshly baked that morning. Not knowing any English, the conversation proceeded over his head.

"You are suggesting that he has met with some sort of misadventure?" her husband asked.

"If that is the case, there has curiously been no reference to him in the media," Marika said. "I have been reading local newspapers and following the television news closely for the last few days."

"One thing is certain," Ivo said. "We can hardly contact the police."

Marika grimaced at the thought.

"What will happen to our young friend here?" she asked.

"Luckily for him," her husband explained, with a glance at the unsuspecting Serb, "he has a girlfriend called Anna working at a hospital in Manchester. We shall have to explain to him, in the unlikely event of Dr. Seifert not showing up within the next few days, that the deal is off. He is not likely to complain, since his main objective was to reach England, which he has now achieved."

"What about payment?"

"I shall give him two hundred pounds to cover his immediate expenses. He is a likeable young fellow and I intend to do the right thing by him. We can't just cast him adrift. In fact, I may drive him to Manchester myself. It's only an hour away."

"It's the least you could do, in the circumstances," Marika agreed, content with her husband's line of thought.

✦　　✦　　✦

That same morning, George Mason joined Chief Inspector Bill Harrington for a routine conference in his office at Scotland Yard.

An assistant served coffee, to which the senior detective added a generous measure of Glen Garioch, his current favorite among single-malt whiskeys.

"What developments in the Seifert case?" he then asked Mason.

"Alison Aubrey and I are giving it our best shot," Mason replied. "But hard facts are proving elusive."

"Which is another way of saying that you've made little or no headway," Harrington groused, "after all the resources already committed to it. Trips to Whalley, Basel, Dresden. Where next?"

George Mason bridled a little at that jibe.

"We're trying to establish Seifert's background and recent contacts," he replied, stiffly. "We've established that he worked at a clinic in Basel, and that his wife Celine died while he was there. There was a trial, during which he was cleared of any responsibility for her death."

"As his wife's physician, you are implying?"

George Mason nodded.

"It was a question of accidental death, self-inflicted overdose, or deliberate poisoning," he explained. "From a prescription painkiller."

"And the jury opted for…?"

"Accidental death."

"Most interesting," Harrington said, softening a little. "By the way, have Seifert's next of kin been informed of his death?"

"If we only knew who they were," Mason said. "No one has so far come forward to state that he is missing. Sergeant Roy Wheeldon has circularized all police stations within a fifty-mile radius of Whalley, without result."

"Where is Seifert now?" the Chief Inspector asked.

"On ice at the Blackburn morgue."

Harrington grimaced at the thought.

"Perhaps his relatives live in Switzerland," he suggested. "You could place a notice in the Basel papers."

"That might not have much result, either," Mason objected. "For one thing, Heini Seifert was not Swiss. He apparently moved to Switzerland from Germany, around the same time his wife Celine's parents moved to England."

"You didn't mention that before."

"I've been meaning to. Celine's parents, Johann and Beate Mueller migrated from Dresden to England shortly after German reunification, modifying their names to John and Betty Miller. They settled in the Lancaster area, not a far cry from the scene of the crime, as a matter of fact."

"Most interesting, Inspector," Harrington considered. "Why, I wonder, would they do that?"

"I imagine they did it to create a fresh start, in a new country, with new names. John Miller was originally a Lutheran clergyman who was jailed in the twilight years of the East German regime."

"For what reason?"

"For alleged subversive activities; namely, helping escapees cross the border near Magdeburg, and involvement in opposition politics."

"So you are thinking, in effect, that he wanted to put all that behind him?"

"That is my reading of the circumstances known to me," Mason said. "One of the chief witnesses against him in court was a certain Heinrich Feldman, whose visiting card was recovered from Seifert's pocket. I was hoping to interview him in Dresden, but he apparently moved elsewhere some years ago."

Bill Harrington sipped his fortified coffee thoughtfully, drumming his fingertips on the walnut desk. After a while, he said:

"What you have here, it seems to me, are parts of a puzzle, but no means as yet of piecing them together. I should think, however, that there is a connection, since everything seems to lead back to the Dresden area. So you have not been wasting departmental resources, after all."

His colleague felt moderately relieved to hear that. It was, as he well knew from previous dealings with his chief over a period of years, Harrington's left-handed way of complimenting him.

"What was Seifert's specialism, as a doctor?" the other then asked.

"Organ transplants."

"Interesting that you should say so, Inspector. The Home Office recently passed on to us a tip they had received from the Ministry of Health about illegal kidney transplants. We have been aware for some quite considerable time that there is at least one Europe-wide network duping poor and needy individuals into sacrificing one of their kidneys for a small pittance. The organs are then sold on to recipients who pay tens of thousands of euros for the privilege."

"Why would the Home Office be involved?" George Mason asked.

"Because they suspect that the network may have reached British shores," came the tart reply. "I am skeptical myself. The Schengen Treaty has abolished passport controls throughout Continental Europe, making it relatively easy for the network to operate from Greece, say, as far as France and Holland. But we still have our Customs officials in place, making it quite difficult to gain illegal entry into Britain."

"Let us hope you are correct in thinking so, Chief Inspector, given the extent of Britain's open coastline."

"I hope so, too, Inspector. Such networks are ruthless. Let us suppose, for a moment, that this Dr. Seifert, a specialist in organ transplants, was somehow involved with that network."

George Mason immediately caught his drift.

"You are suggesting that he may have fallen foul of the system, in some way, and been eliminated," he said. "I think that's a long shot, given the evidence we have so far."

"But you could treat it as a working hypothesis," Harrington said, "especially since you do not appear to have an alternative reading of the case. It might mean a second trip to Switzerland to find out more about Seifert's background. You might also place a notice in the newspaper, inviting people who knew him to contact you by box number."

"I'll place it in *Basler Zeitung*," his colleague said, inwardly pleased at Harrington's proposition.

On returning to his own office, he met with Detective Sergeant Aubrey, whom he informed of his chief's line of thinking. Alison was not over-surprised about the activities of an illegal organ network, even while professing skepticism that it had reached Britain. She told Mason she had read that in some countries they even went so far as to execute criminals, expressly to remove their vital organs for sale on the black market.

"My goodness!" was Mason's sole reaction, wondering what the world was coming to.

Chapter Five

Rachel Slade left home early, dropping her two children off at school before driving to her costume jewelry boutique near Blackpool's north shore. Her husband Craig had left an hour earlier, to start the morning shift at the public utility company where he was employed as a maintenance supervisor. That involved leading a crew to inspect and repair power lines over a broad area of the northwest, from the Fylde coast to the Lake District. It had been an exacting job of late, owing to a spate of unseasonal heavy storms, which had left some towns without power for several days. As she drove up the coast road, in view of the Golden Mile of uninterrupted sand that would soon draw thousands of visitors, she noted that the sea was still quite rough from the storm last night, with heavy breakers crashing up against the sea-wall. Always fascinated by the moods of the sea, she stopped her car briefly to watch the heavy spray shoot up into the air and the gulls buffeted by the wind, congratulating herself on her decision to relocate here from the market town of Preston, some distance to the south.

It had been a wise move from a business point of view. Her boutique sold costume jewelry and wardrobe accessories to suit everybody's price-range, from junk to high-end. It had prospered from its location in one of England's top tourist spots. Although in recent decades Britons had tended to head south in summer to the beaches of France and Spain and their more dependable weather, Blackpool had retained its loyal devotees, if nowadays mainly for weekend breaks. She put that down to a tradition deeply-rooted in the industrial towns of the region. Long before Continental holidays grew popular along with higher standards of living, and long before air travel became the norm, workers in the offices, factories and mills of Lancashire and beyond took their annual two-week vacation on the west coast. They arrived by steam train, mainly to Blackpool, but also to Lytham St. Anne's, the fishing port of Fleetwood and Southport, whose Victorian shopping arcades also drew year-round visitors. She was planning to open a second boutique in the fall, but had found it difficult to decide between Southport and Lytham, thinking that the latter might provide more well-heeled customers.

Parking her Audi in the main square, she approached her business premises on foot, unlocked the front door, but left the security grille over the display window in place. Wednesday was usually a quiet day, since most small businesses, apart from food stores, closed at noon, to compensate retailers for full-day opening on Saturdays. Rachel Slade had today decided to take the morning off as well, needing only to make a few phone calls to suppliers for the cheaper lines of stock that would be in more demand with summer week-enders and those unable to afford holidays abroad. In the winter months, she relied on her high-end trade. There were political conventions and business dinners at the resort's leading hotels, for example, and civic functions where the wives of dignitaries needed to make an impression. And, of course, there was Christmas, which had always been good for all categories of her trade.

Completing her task within the hour, she returned to her car and drove eastwards across the Fylde towards Goosenargh, experiencing a sudden frisson as she passed its medieval hall, said to be the most haunted building in Britain. A short drive from there brought her to Longridge, where she stopped for coffee and a bite to eat, having skimped breakfast to get her children to school on time. The interior of the café, situated in a row of stone-fronted buildings overlooking Longridge Fell, was cheerful and inviting, with soft floral fabrics and the smell of freshly-baked rolls. In no particular hurry, she took time during her brief refreshment to flick through the travel brochures she had brought with her, singling out the one on Zurich for a closer reading. Never having been to that city, she was keenly looking forward to visiting the trade fair to be held there, in a guildhall beside the River Limmat. From the detailed map of the compact city center, she found its precise location and figured out how to reach it from the Hauptbahnhof, where she would arrive by rail link from Kloten Airport. Not particularly interested in tourist amenities and cultural offerings – she could discover those for herself on arrival – she then scanned the list of hotels, opting for Der Hirsch in the Altstadt, whose charges seemed relatively modest. Relative was the operative word, she reflected, given the high cost of living in Switzerland.

Before leaving Longridge, she called in at the travel agency farther along the main street, where she booked a return flight and three nights in a single room at her chosen hotel. She regretted that Craig could not accompany her on this occasion, as he had on previous similar trips to Paris and Milan. His utility company was behind schedule with maintenance work and, even though his sister living nearby would look after their children, there was no way he could arrange leave at short notice. A pity, she considered, because she was rather loathe to travel solo, since it involved lonely nights in hotel rooms, solo dinners in unfamiliar restaurants and the synthetic bonhomie among participants in the fair.

On leaving the travel agency, however, she quickly shrugged off negative feelings and concentrated on the task ahead. Wasn't she a successful businesswoman in her own right, she asked herself?

Someone quite capable of rising to whatever challenge presented itself? Wasn't she the sort of new woman who was perfectly able to function without the support of a male presence, a shoulder to cry on, and all that pre-feminist nonsense? Glancing in the car vanity mirror to adjust her short blond fringe and re-touch her lipstick, she saw a confident young woman in her late twenties, with the world before, smiling approvingly back at her. Turning the key in the ignition, she headed down the winding country road, noting here and there a pheasant by a hawthorn hedge or a plover in the open sky. The pleasantly scenic route took her through the picturesque villages of Hurst Green, where she had betimes enjoyed family dinners at The Shireburn Arms, and Great Mytton towards Clitheroe, where she had more business to attend to.

+   +   +

When George Mason arrived in Basel later that same day, he went straight away to the offices of *Basler Zeitung*, placing a notice in Obituaries announcing Heini Seifert's decease. In the Personal column he placed a second notice, inviting people who knew the doctor to contact him in writing via a box number. That done, he re-threaded his way through the busy streets to the Hauptbahnhof, where he caught the next train to Zurich, buying a copy of the London *Times* to read on the way. He arrived at his destination mid-afternoon, making his way on foot to Hotel Fiedler on the Niederdorf, where he had pre-booked a room. The fascinating narrow street running parallel to the Limmatquai was full of its usual hustle and bustle: street vendors hawking their wares; tourists jostling each other; aromas of grilled bratwurst, beer and roasted snails; an accordionist playing native and gypsy melodies. Had he ever strolled down another street like it, he wondered, in all his travels?

On registering at Reception, he mounted the creaking wooden staircase to his second-floor room, where he immediately poured himself a scotch-and-soda from the minibar, planting himself in the easy chair for a while, to relax and watch the television news. He regretted that Alison Aubrey was unable to accompany him on this occasion; he would miss her lively personality, shrewd input and feminine intuition. Chief Inspector Harrington had switched her temporarily to a new case in the Metropolitan Area, on the grounds that the Yard was short-handed. The reality, Mason suspected, was more likely to be shortage of funds, since the police service, in common with most government agencies, had not escaped deep cut-backs occasioned by the recession. Harrington had assured him that the young detective sergeant would be able to rejoin the case at a later stage.

It was almost five o'clock when, after a quick shower, he quit the hotel and made his way down a cobbled side-street to the Limmat embankment. Crossing the river by the bridge near the Wasserkirche, flanked by a statue of Protestant reformer Ulrich Zwingli, he proceeded along the covered arcade housing quaint-looking boutiques. They specialized in paintings, prints and maps, wood sculpture, jewelry, ceramics or art glass. He paused now and then to admire the arresting window displays, as ever amazed at the extent of human ingenuity, artistry and craftsmanship. If only the price-tags were a little lower, he mused, to accommodate a policeman's salary. By the time he reached the Polizei Dienst, Leutnant Rudi Kubler, whom the Scotland Yard detective had phoned before leaving London to alert him of his visit, was just finishing his day shift.

"Delighted to meet you again, Inspektor," the Swiss officer declared, emerging from behind his desk to shake his visitor's hand vigorously. "What nefarious business brings you back to Zurich?"

"A murder case," George Mason replied, "with possible Swiss ramifications."

"Indeed?" came the surprised reaction. "And we are such a peace-loving nation!"

"The crime took place in England," Mason wryly replied.

Leutnant Kubler made a half-hearted attempt at clearing his cluttered desk, returning key documents to a filing cabinet, before leading the way out of police headquarters.

"A crime involving a Swiss citizen?" he asked, as they made their way along nearby Bahnhofstrasse, the city's main thoroughfare.

"The victim was formerly a resident of Basel," Mason explained. "But I suspect he originally came from Germany."

"That's very possible, Inspektor. But how about a bite to eat, while you describe the case to me? I expect you're quite hungry after your trip."

The detective found no objection to that proposal, keeping in step with his Swiss counterpart as he took a left turn into one of the side-streets that led from Bahnhofstrasse into the Altstadt, the old quarter of the city dating from Roman times. Their path grew steeper and narrower, until the lieutenant eventually stopped outside a small *Stube* fronted with small panes of a greenish dimpled glass.

"Die Reben," he announced. "One of my favorite eateries. I occasionally call here after work, especially if my wife is working overtime."

They entered, found a quiet corner table in the paneled interior and scanned the menu, ordering *Rindfillets mit frites* or, to the Englishman's way of thinking, fillets of beef with chips. To help it down, they requested steins of the local Hurlimann's ale, speedily served by the buxom waitress.

"Inspektor Mason," Rudi Kubler began, after a satisfying quaff, "I well recall the invaluable assistance you gave to my department some years ago, in helping us expose The Amadeo Agenda. Anything I can do to help in your current case, you have only to ask."

"I am really just looking for a few pointers," the grateful detective replied.

"Fire away, then."

"It concerns the victim, mainly. I have been trying to build a picture of his background and contacts, to establish a possible motive for his murder."

"His name?"

"Heini Seifert," Mason informed him. "He worked as a surgeon performing organ transplants at Klinik Mauser in Basel."

"But you claim he was from Germany?"

"So the clinic told me."

"That's rather curious," Kubler considered, "since that is a typically Swiss name."

"I am wondering how I can get a clearer picture of his background."

The Swiss officer thought about that, as they addressed their attention to the meal, newly-served.

"If Seifert became a Swiss resident," Kubler said, after a while, "his application would have been closely vetted by Immigration. They would certainly be able to tell you his place of birth and similar details."

"Such as?" the curious visitor enquired.

The lieutenant noisily cleared his throat and added, rather sheepishly:

"His financial means, for one thing. Did you know that an applicant for permanent residence in Switzerland must have assets of at least 200,000 francs?"

"That would rule out a lot of people," Mason remarked, "including myself, if I ever wished to retire here."

Rudi Kubler returned an indulgent smile.

"But it would not necessarily rule out a German surgeon," he said. "You should go to the Immigration Bureau and find out what you can."

"But will they disclose such information to a foreigner?"

"They will if I give you a letter of introduction," the other replied. "Call round at my office first thing tomorrow morning. I shall have it ready by nine o'clock."

"I appreciate that, Leutnant."

"Just routine, Inspektor. Only too pleased to be of help."

"The Immigration Bureau," Mason then said, "is presumably in the federal capital?"

"In Bern," came the immediate reply. "The precise address escapes me for the moment. You could look it up on the computer at your hotel."

To round off their meal, they ordered strudels and coffee, as the inviting *Stube* began to fill with early diners like themselves. A cuckoo clock on the wall above their table announced the hour, quite startling the English visitor by its unexpectedness.

"I'm still rather curious about the victim's name," Rudi Kubler said. "Quite a few people moved here from East Germany soon after reunification in 1990."

"To Switzerland, rather than to West Germany?" a surprised George Mason asked.

"To Switzerland, and also to Austria or Holland, where they would have fewer language problems. Less so to France and Italy. Some of them, in my view, may have done so to avoid reprisals."

"Can you be more specific?"

"The German Democratic Republic operated by a system of informers," the lieutenant said. "To keep people in line and loyal to the state, co-workers, associates and even members of families were encouraged to spy on each other and report suspicious activities, questionable attitudes or merely loose remarks, to the authorities. The Stasi then became involved and thousands of people were imprisoned. That created a deal of resentment, ill will and scores to settle after the collapse of the Communist regime."

"You mean that some informers got out while they could and settled in a different country, changing their names in the process?" The Reverend Johann Mueller came to his mind, but he was surely more sinned against than sinner. More relevant, perhaps, was Heinrich Feldman, who had disappeared off the radar.

"You get my meaning perfectly," Kubler said, with an acid smile.

George Mason sipped his coffee thoughtfully, at the conclusion of his meal, congratulating himself on having approached his old contact. The wily lieutenant, being closer to the source of these events, knew far more about the Stasi and their doings than Scotland Yard ever would.

"I'll drop by first thing tomorrow morning," Mason said, as they settled their bill and rose to leave.

"The letter of introduction will be waiting for you," the Swiss officer promised.

After they parted company, George Mason threaded his way through the cobbled streets of the Altstadt to the embankment, tracing the river back to the point where it flowed out of the lake. It was still light at that hour, so he took advantage of the fine evening to stroll along the strand to watch the yachts tacking across the water, against a backdrop of snow-capped peaks to the south. On reaching the large beer garden near Belle Vue, he remained there for a while to smoke one of his Dutch cigars. As dusk descended, a group of musicians began playing dance music. Colored fairy lights came on, festooning the open-air dance-floor and creating a romantic aura for the few young couples wishing to shake a leg. It was quite dark when he eventually reached his hotel, buying a nightcap in the bar-lounge to enjoy while he finished reading the *Times*, mainly to catch up on Barclay's Premier League soccer scores.

Next day, he was up early for a breakfast of muesli and yoghurt with a glass of *apfelsaft*, followed by poached-eggs-on-toast and strong coffee. After making a quick phone call to his wife Adele, to ascertain that all was well on the home front, he walked briskly down to the Polizei Dienst, conferred briefly with Leutnant Kubler, gratefully pocketed the letter of introduction and proceeded to the Hauptbahnhof. The trip by *Schnellzug*, via Olten and Langenthal, took exactly two hours, bringing him to his destination just before midday. With the aid of a rough street-plan copied from the hotel computer, he soon located the Immigration Bureau in a row of official buildings fronting the River Aare. Entering, he approached the enquiry desk and was directed to an office facing the river, where he handed Kubler's letter to the duty clerk. The latter, an elderly man with rimless spectacles, perused it carefully and fixed an inquisitive gaze on the visitor.

"Scotland Yard?" he asked, much intrigued.

George Mason nodded.

"What exactly is it that you wish to learn?"

"If possible," the detective replied, "I wish to discover the date when a Dr. Heini Seifert was granted permanent residence in Switzerland, and also his place of origin."

"Then you have come to the right place," the helpful clerk said, turning towards a large filing cabinet to his rear. After a brief search, he withdrew a buff-colored folder, which he opened and spread on the desk. "Dr. Seifert received his residence permit from this office on July 2nd, 1990."

"Arriving from…?" Mason prompted.

"Dresden," came the reply.

"Do you have anything else on him?"

The clerk flicked quickly through the folder.

"He changed his name by deed poll," he said. "Which is in the public domain, so there are no restrictions on my divulging it."

The detective held his breath, with a keen sense of anticipation. The clerk answered his enquiring gaze.

"His birth name was Heinrich Feldman," he said, matter-of-factly.

George Mason took a step backwards and gasped in astonishment. A number of things at once became clearer to him, after what Rolf Kubler had told him last evening, as he thanked the clerk and hurried back to the station to grab a bite to eat before catching the train to Basel. So Heinrich Feldman and Heini Seifert were one and the same person! What a turn-up for the book! If Heinrich

Feldman had been a Stasi informer, that would have been sufficient reason to adopt a new identity on reaching Switzerland, to cover his tracks. He may well have made enemies, any one of whom might have sought revenge over the intervening years. The question now was to identify that individual who had sufficient motive to kill him, someone with a long memory leading back more than twenty years. Biting into an Emmental cheese roll in the station buffet, and slaking a growing thirst with a large glass of *apfelsaft*, the detective was suddenly struck full-force by another aspect of this intriguing case. John and Betty Millers' daughter Celine had married the very person who had caused her family so much grief! It would take him some time, he considered, as the arrival of the Geneva-Bern-Basel express was announced over the loudspeaker, to figure out the logic of that. Quickly finishing his snack, he sprinted towards Platform 2, making his connection in the nick of time.

On arrival in Basel three hours later, he took a taxi to Hotel Balade, where he and Alison Aubrey had stayed on the previous visit. He was pleased to find that he was given the same room; it made him feel more at home. Helping himself to a whiskey-and-soda from the minibar, he relaxed for a short while before venturing out, aiming to reach the offices of *Basler Zeitung* before they closed for the day. On arrival there shortly before five o'clock, he collected quite a number of replies to his announcement in the Personal column inviting people who knew Heini Seifert to contact him. Since it was a moderately fine evening, with rain clouds threatening from the south, he found a café with outdoor tables overlooking the Rhine, ordered lemon tea and a Danish pastry to tide him over until dinner, and opened his box-number mail. The first few letters were from the doctor's former patients, outlining what he had done for them, while expressing both surprise and regret at his untimely death and conveying condolences to his survivors. If only he knew who those were!

The last two replies he read had more potential, for professional purposes. One was from a certain Freni Kusnacht, who wrote that she assuredly wished to know more details of the doctor's death, over and above the brief announcement in the newspaper. To that end she supplied a telephone number in the Basel area, requesting the earliest possible meeting. The final response was from the manager of Bank Linus Vogelin, a certain Maurice Behrens, who wrote that he had seen the notice in Obituaries and needed to contact heirs to Seifert's estate regarding sums held on deposit. To that end, he also gave a local telephone number and the information that the branch where the account was held was situated almost directly opposite the Hauptbahnhof. George Mason checked his watch. It was just turned six o'clock and, since banks closed at five, he would not be able to contact the banker until morning. Rising from his seat with a sense of guarded satisfaction at these developments, he entered the interior of the café and asked to use the telephone. Getting the engaged tone, he returned to his table, finished his snack and waited another ten minutes before trying again.

"Hallo?" came a soft female voice on the end of the line.

"*Guten Abend*," the detective said, in his best German. "George Mason, from England. You replied to my recent announcement in *Basler Zeitung*."

"Regarding Dr. Seifert," the woman said, eagerly. "I was truly surprised to learn of his death. But why are you here from England?"

"I'll explain things, if we can meet. You indicated in your letter that you wished to discuss certain matters."

"I would assuredly wish to know the details," came the reply. "Dr. Seifert and I were very close friends."

"Do you happen to be free this evening?" the detective asked.

The woman seemed to hesitate.

"I have a choir rehearsal with Basler Kantorei at seven," she said.

"Can you skip it on this occasion?" Mason asked. "I'm only in Basel briefly."

"Very well," she replied, still rather hesitantly. "I could afford to miss the first half, which is a re-cap of last week's material."

"Could you perhaps join me for an early dinner at, say, six-thirty?"

"I could do that, as I haven't eaten yet. As a matter of fact, I usually eat out somewhere in town on rehearsal nights. Whereabouts are you, exactly?"

"Over by the newspaper office. I was planning to visit a riverside restaurant opposite Schifflande. I don't know Basel very well, but I have eaten there before."

"I know the place you mean. They have a classical pianist and serve traditional Swiss dishes. Let us say a quarter to seven, Mr. Mason. It will take me a little while to reach you from my end of town."

George Mason replaced the receiver, thanked the café owner and directed his steps towards Schifflande, to spend the interval observing the river traffic, feeling upbeat at the prospect of at last meeting someone who actually knew the deceased. What sort of person would this Freni Kusnacht turn out to be, he wondered? She sounded a fairly cultured type on the telephone and spoke English well, as did most educated Swiss. Her presence at dinner would at the very least make up for the absence of Alison Aubrey, affording him up to two hours of female company. After a half-hour or so of watching the boats as the sky grew overcast, he entered the restaurant, occupying a table for two near the entrance. He did not wait long, just long enough in fact to order an aperitif, when a tall, elegant female appeared in the doorway, clasping in one hand what he immediately noted was a Bruckner score. He rose to greet her.

"Frau Kusnacht?" he enquired, genially.

"*Fraulein* Kusnacht," she emphasized, grasping his outstretched hand.

"George Mason," the detective said.

Introductions completed, they took their seats and appraised each other carefully. Mason took her to be someone in her early fifties, whose auburn hair was tied back, highlighting the contours of her face. She wore little make-up, her complexion having a freshness that suggested an outdoor life. She placed the score face-up beside her.

"Rehearsing the *Te Deum?*" he asked, with interest.

Freni raised her eyes from the menu and smiled.

"You are familiar with Bruckner's music?" she asked.

"A nodding acquaintance, no more than that."

His interest in her choral activities broke the ice. They chatted amiably for a while about musical matters, the detective recalling his contribution to St. Wilfrid's choir in Zurich some time ago and the Vaughan Williams program he had persuaded Leutnant Rolf Kubler and his wife to attend at the successful conclusion of a joint investigation. The waitress appeared minutes later to serve raclettes with an endive side-salad. They chose a dry white wine from the Valais to help it down, as the resident pianist launched on his evening program.

"Now please tell me about Heini," Freni said, having consciously deferred discussion of a delicate matter until after they had eaten.

George Mason felt that frankness was the best policy.

"We are treating his death as a murder case," he said, observing her reaction closely.

Freyni Kusnacht gasped and sat back in disbelief, a look of anguish crossing her features.

"You can't be serious!" she exclaimed.

"I am only too serious," he replied. "Let me explain. I am a detective from Scotland Yard in charge of the investigation."

"Scotland Yard!" she exclaimed, breaking into a nervous laugh at the seeming incongruity of her situation. "I am actually being interviewed by someone from Scotland Yard?"

"Interviewed, but not interrogated," Mason hastened to reassure her. He re-filled her wine glass, partly to calm her nerves, partly to ease her tongue.

She raised the glass, fixing her dark-brown eyes upon him, warily.

"You were evidently close friends," he then said, "judging from your reaction."

"We were more than that," she guardedly replied.

"Lovers?"

Freni slowly nodded, but the detective's taut features registered no reaction at the disclosure.

"That would be some time ago," he enquired, "before he moved to England?"

"I broke off the relationship some time before he went to England," a more-at-ease Freni explained.

"Do you mind telling me the reason?"

She took another sip of wine, glanced quickly at her watch to make sure she was all right for time, and said:

"Did you know that Heini Seifert was involved in a major trial?"

"I read a report of it in *Basler Zeitung*," he replied. "Did you attend?"

Freni Kusnacht nodded.

"And what was your reaction?"

"I thought, considering all the circumstances, that he was guilty. Heini was Celine's physician and, as such, responsible for her medications. I think he poisoned her."

"What makes you say that?" he enquired.

"Their relationship had soured, as a result of Celine's skiing injury and consequent depressive illness. It wasn't helped by the death of their son in a motoring accident."

"They had a son?"

"Manfred," came the reply. "He was a medical student at the university here."

"That must have been quite a serious blow to them," Mason observed.

"I think it was the final straw," she sadly replied. "I also think that Heini saw a way out of a difficult relationship and decided to take it. He managed to get away with it, too. As you no doubt read in the trial report, he was acquitted."

"I do so recall," Mason said, in turn glancing at his watch. "By the way, I hope I'm not keeping you from your choir?"

"The venue is quite close by," Freni replied. "We still have time. I could, however, use a strong coffee after all the wine, to clear my head."

"Dessert?"

She declined, so Mason promptly ordered two black coffees.

"Did the Seifferts have other children?" he asked.

"They also had a daughter," Freni told him. "But I believe she became estranged from her father. My guess is that she too thought he was guilty."

"Her name?"

"It escapes me for the moment. I never actually met her, and I only met Manfred Seifert on one occasion, at an exhibition of Picasso drawings in the Zurich Kunsthalle, the year before his death."

George Mason sat back to enjoy his coffee and absorb this new information. They both listened to the pianist for a while. He had resumed after a brief interval, playing Chopin waltzes. His companion flicked briefly through her music score, as if mentally rehearsing key passages.

"What prompted Dr. Seifert's move to England?" he then asked.

Freni quickly closed the score, assuming a pensive look.

"I think his main motivation was to make a fresh start," she replied, "to put the trial and everything associated with it, and with Celine and their son Manfred, in the past. He had already opened a facility there some time before he retired from Klinik Mauser, dividing his time between the two."

"Did you maintain contact with him?"

"Only to the extent of exchanging Christmas greetings."

"So you would know his most recent address?" George Mason asked, quickly seizing on this key piece of information.

"Wellman Clinic, Clitheroe, Lancashire," she replied, without hesitation. "I cannot tell you the postcode off-hand, but I have it written down somewhere."

The detective made a note of it, keenly aware that Clitheroe was not many miles from Whalley.

"So he continued in medical practise?" he said.

"I believe so."

"Might there have been other reasons for his move?" Mason asked.

"Heini had, for some time, been receiving threatening letters. He never told me in much detail what prompted them, but I gradually formed the impression that they were connected to his former life in Dresden. He was born in that city and lived there many years before moving to Switzerland."

George Mason promptly fished inside his wallet, producing the visiting card recovered from the victim's body. He passed it across the table, but noticed no discernable reaction other than puzzlement.

"Heinrich Feldman, M.D.," she remarked. "Should this name mean something to me?"

"It was Heini Seifert's birth name," the detective said. "He changed it by deed poll on arrival in this country."

"You truly amaze me, Inspector," Freni said. "How could you have possibly known a thing like that?"

"Professional sources," he diffidently replied, conscious that it was Leutnant Rolf Kubler who had prompted that particular line of enquiry.

"The person who was threatening him must therefore have known of his change of name?" she said.

The detective agreed.

"Were the threats regarding legal action, or of causing actual physical harm?" he asked.

"They were sufficient to cause Heini grave concern, I do know that," Freni said. "But, perhaps to spare me anxiety, he never really opened up about them. It may well have been that they were threats to his life."

The detective drummed with his fingertips on the table, in time with the mazurka the pianist was now playing, wondering if he should tell the woman what he knew of Heinrich Feldman's past. She forestalled him.

"I think he may have made enemies in East Germany," she said. "Life there under the Communist regime was no picnic."

"You can say that again," Mason remarked, breaking into a smile at her choice of words.

Freni Kusnacht smiled too, easing what had hitherto been a fairly tense atmosphere.

"You would not know then," he said, "that Heini Seifert, alias Heinrich Feldman, was a Stasi informer?"

The woman gasped, almost spilling her coffee.

"Or that his deceased wife Celine was the daughter of a prominent cleric he had helped put behind bars?"

The woman regarded him in disbelief.

"Now you must really be off-target," she objected. "How could a situation like that possibly have arisen?"

George Mason sat back and returned an ironic smile, slightly amused at the effect of his words.

"From what I gather," he replied, "many odd things that may not have happened in, say, Britain or Switzerland, took place in the German Democratic Republic. Families were often divided against themselves. The secret police were everywhere. The walls had ears."

"That, regretfully Mr. Mason, was very true, and I shall take your word for everything you have told me this evening. And a very informative evening it has been, without a doubt. Now, if you will excuse me, choir duty calls."

With that, she gathered her music score and got up to leave.

The detective rose to his feet, thanked her for her company and bade her a successful rehearsal.

"You have my phone number," she said, "in case I can be of further help."

After she had left, he stayed put, ordering a refill of coffee while mulling over what his table companion had told him. The threatening letters she had mentioned provided clear evidence that someone was out to harm Heini Seifert, and that his death could most likely be traced back to his activities in Dresden. Yet there was no indication of who the author of those letters was. Another curious fact was the existence of an estranged daughter, wherever she might be. At least he now had an address in Clitheroe, which he would waste no time in visiting as soon as he got back to England. Feeling that the case was moving forward, even if slowly and hesitantly, he ordered a cognac to complement his coffee, while waiting for the pianist to complete his program. At the next break in the performance, he settled his bill and returned to Hotel Balade for a good night's sleep.

Next day, straight after breakfast, he placed a call to Bank Linus Vogelin, which he imagined to be one of those private investment banks so sought after by tax evaders in Britain and other European countries. The receptionist put him through to the manager, Herr Behrens.

"*Guten Tag*," he said, using his best German. "Let me introduce myself. I am George Mason from London, ringing about your response to my recent notice in *Basler Zeitung*."

"*Guten Tag*, Herr Mason," came the prompt reply. "You are no doubt ringing in connection with the death of Dr. Heini Seifert?"

"To arrange a meeting, if possible."

"Yes, I think that would be in order," the banker said, rather pompously. "Now let me see…er…I shall be tied up with an important client for the next hour or so. Could we make it at, say, 11 a.m.?"

"At your premises?"

"Bank Linus Vogelin, almost directly opposite the Hauptbahnhof."

"I shall be there," Mason confirmed.

"*Bis spater*," the banker said, ringing off.

Later that morning suited the detective, allowing him the opportunity to do some personal shopping in the downtown area. He next rang his wife Adele, to enquire how her bridge session had gone last evening – she had recently joined a neighborhood group as a comparative novice – as well as to inform her that he expected to arrive home later that day. Adele considered her card evening to have been a qualified success and promised to keep dinner back until he arrived home. With a mid-afternoon flight in prospect, he checked out of the hotel and proceeded on foot to the Hauptbahnhof, to deposit his valise ahead of his rail connection to the airport, before attending to the morning's business. A few minutes before eleven o'clock, he presented himself at the premises of Bank Linus Vogelin, where he was shown immediately into the conference room.

"Please do take a seat, Herr Mason," the banker said, appearing through a door to his private office, "while I order fresh coffee."

Left to himself for a few moments, the detective took stock of his surroundings. It was about the plushest office he had ever visited, a far cry from the more Spartan, budget-conscious amenities at Scotland Yard. Seated in a red, leather-upholstered chair before a highly-polished rosewood table, his curious gaze scanned what he took to be a series of Corot landscapes – originals, he wondered? – lining the paneled walls. A mineral water fountain occupied one corner, next to a large screen used for film-projection. Dark-red velvet drapes hung at the tall windows, beyond which he espied window boxes with spring blooms. If this was private banking, he mused, it had a lot to commend it, revising upwards his estimate of Dr. Seifert's means.

Maurice Behrens entered and took the seat immediately to Mason's left.

"I was very surprised, Herr Mason," he began, "to learn of Dr. Seifert's death. He seemed in the pink of health last time we met."

"He did not die of natural causes," his visitor explained. "We are treating his death as a case of murder."

The banker's face registered both dismay and disbelief.

"You can't be serious," he replied.

"Let me explain myself, Herr Behrens," the detective said. "I am Inspector George Mason, of Scotland Yard Special Branch. I am here to investigate a crime committed in northwest England about two weeks ago."

"The victim being… Dr. Seifert?" the other hesitantly enquired.

"I am afraid so."

"And what is it you wish to know, Herr Inspektor?"

"First of all, your reason for answering my newspaper notice."

"I did so for the simple reason that the deceased held an account at this branch. There arises the question of how to proceed with disposal of his assets. In other words, who his heirs are and their legal respresentatives."

"What sort of sums are we talking about?" Mason enquired.

"I am not at liberty to disclose actual amounts, Inspektor Mason," the banker evasively replied, "on account of our banking secrecy laws. I feel sure you can appreciate that. But I am able to disclose that our minimum balance is 500,000 Swiss francs."

The detective raised eyebrows at that remark. A fuller picture of the assets on deposit would throw light on Seifert's medical practice. In view of what surgeons in the National Health Service typically earned, few of them would be expected to amass substantial wealth, unless they were also named in the wills of affluent patients. Still, an account worth over half a million francs at an institution like this, pointed to some lucrative activities on the part of the deceased surgeon.

"Am I not correct in thinking, Herr Behrens," he continued,

on a different tack, "that a new agreement is now in force requiring Swiss banks to deduct income tax owed in Britain on monies transferred abroad?"

"That is certainly true, Herr Inspektor."

"Which in itself compromises your vaunted secrecy laws."

"Taxation matters are a confidential matter between ourselves and UK Inland Revenue. If you require information on that score, you should contact them directly to determine the tax status, or non-status, of the deceased."

Coffee and strudels were served at that point, by a smartly-dressed young female assistant, who bestowed on the detective an engaging smile. While his host did the honors, enquiring if his visitor took cream and sugar, George Mason pondered that last remark. Was Behrens implying that Seifert may not have had a tax status in Britain; that he in fact had been evading income tax on UK earnings by means of his Swiss account?

"On the understanding that Dr. Seifert transferred moneys from Britain," Mason resumed, after a brief hiatus, "can you tell me the source and frequency of those transfers?"

"Again, Inspektor Mason," the banker replied, "those are not matters I could in all sincerity discuss. It may strike you as odd, but we take confidentiality issues very seriously. Our government, in fact, requires it."

The Scotland Yard man sipped his coffee, thoughtfully.

"This coffee is first-rate," he commented, with the growing feeling that he was going to leave the premises with little beyond the suspicion that the deceased had been a comparatively wealthy man. That knowledge in itself was at least worth something.

"It's from our Java estates," the other proudly proclaimed. "But please, do also help yourself to a strudel. They're freshly-baked."

The visitor, thinking of his waistline, had been meaning to resist the temptation, but the banker's prompt was sufficient to persuade him otherwise. Maurice Behrens, himself abstemious, looked on appreciatively as his visitor ate.

"Dr. Seifert's death," he then said, "raises the question of beneficiaries. Do you have any information on that score?"

"Afraid not," his visitor replied, between mouthfuls. "No one has so far come forward even to claim his remains."

"That raises an interesting legal point," the banker said. "If no claim is made to Seifert's estate within five years, his assets revert to the Swiss government."

George Mason raised eyebrows at that remark, wondering if that particular provision did not date back to World War 2, when billions in assets lying in bank accounts would have gone unclaimed, for a variety of reasons, some of which no doubt concerned the fate of the Jews. But he tactfully did not press the point, as he nudged his plate aside and wiped his lips on an ultra-soft tissue.

"I fully expect someone will emerge out of the shadows within that time-frame," he jocularly remarked. "Five years is quite a long time, and I do know that he had a daughter, from whom he became estranged."

"I was not aware of that," the banker said. "But I did know he had a son who lost his life in a motoring accident."

"Seifert did not, by any chance, leave a copy of his will in your keeping?" the detective asked, trying a different approach.

Maurice Behrens shook his head, regretfully.

"So what is the position now, with regard to the deceased's assets held at this bank?"

"His account here will be frozen, until we hear either from a designated heir, or from that person's appointed legal representative."

"If any party does happen to contact you in the future regarding this estate, would you be kind enough to inform me?" Mason asked, handing him his card.

"I can certainly do that," the banker replied, glancing briefly at it before placing it in his wallet. "I wonder what will become of his whiskey collection?"

"I beg your pardon?" a bemused George Mason asked.

"Dr. Seifert was an avid collector of single malts," came the reply. "He had several bottles as much as thirty years old. It was an interest we had in common, except that I concentrate on brandies and liqueurs."

"His heirs then, whoever they may be," the detective quipped, "will have a pleasant surprise in store. Chief Inspector Harrington, back at the yard, is also a devotee of the single malt."

"An interesting coincidence," Maurice Behrens agreed.

Chapter Six

"**I** shall expect you back for dinner," Marika Grigorev told her husband, as he prepared mid-morning to leave Clitheroe in his brand-new VW Jetta.

"By six at the very latest," Ivo replied. "It will take me about an hour each way, plus time to locate Anna's address. After that, I shall be meeting Radko for a late lunch."

"Radko?" a puzzled Marika enquired.

"The guy who runs the filling stations," her husband said. "It's mainly to catch up on how some of our previous donors have fared. Whether they have moved on and integrated into English society."

"That is worth doing," his young wife agreed. "That way, we make sure there are no loose ends, no problems that can surface at a later stage. We can draw a line under this whole business and retire to the South of France."

"I thought you preferred Tuscany," Ivo quipped, with a rather impish look.

"Tuscany, Antibes, Malaga…what difference does it make, so long as we enjoy almost constant sunshine?"

"We'll discuss it further over dinner, Marika," he said, turning the key in the ignition. "But whatever we decide, we must act soon."

"What about Zivko?" she anxiously asked.

"He will fend for himself. I can't pay Radko his usual cut for the simple reason that the transplant did not take place. Besides, Zivko can count on his girl, Anna, who has a good job with the National Health Service."

Marika smiled complaisantly, reassured that Ivo had all the answers, as the young Serb emerged from the clinic with a packed suitcase and clambered into the front passenger seat. He waved good-bye to a woman who had done her best, these last few days, to make him feel at home in a strange country, even to the extent of teaching him some basic English. He was pleased, on the whole, that the transplant did not take place as planned. His organs were intact and, thanks to Ivo, he was two hundred English pounds to the good and about to start on a new life. As the car headed towards Whalley, he had the opportunity to admire the beauty of the local countryside, its meadows, copses, gleaming rivers and small farms where horses, cattle or sheep contentedly grazed. Was there anywhere, he wondered, a greener or gentler landscape? Thereafter, their route led through the industrial town of Accrington, before they joined the dual-carriageway heading south.

Manchester, which they reached around noon, had so far meant just one thing to Zivko Plesijc. It was the home of Barclays Premier League champions Manchester United, the world-famous soccer club that had scores of fans, courtesy of television, even on his native turf. They had even played against Belgrade in the European Cup, causing conflicted loyalties. As Ivo carefully negotiated the traffic in the busy city center, he had time to admire the neo-Gothic architecture of the town hall on Albert Square and the neo-Classic library on St. Peter's Square, before they turned into Oxford Road, heading out past the university to the address in Longsight that Anna had given him. On reaching it, with help from a mailman, Ivo drew up outside a building towards one end of a row of large Victorian dwellings, their once-elegant stonework blackened by decades of soot from factories and domestic fires. As Zivko made to step out with his few belongings, his driver shook his hand with genuine warmth and wished him luck. The car then did a U-turn in the narrow street and sped off towards Radko's premises on the northern rim of the city.

Zivko approached the main door of 93 Cheviot Street, placed his suitcase on the stone step and nervously rang the bell. He had been hoping on the drive from Clitheroe that Anna would be there to greet him. But he was also aware that she worked shifts at the hospital and could equally be still on duty; in which event, he hoped to be admitted to her apartment to await her return. There being no immediate reply to his summons, he pressed the doorbell again, holding it longer. He could hear it ring loudly behind the stout wooden door, but again there was no answer. He stepped back and gazed up at the second-storey windows, draped in faded lace. There was no sign of life. He stepped back into the street. The adjoining houses in the Victorian terrace seemed just as quiet, leading the young Serb to think that everyone must be still at work. A glance at his watch told him that it was twelve-thirty. He had a whole afternoon to kill and he felt hungry. He would spend time, he considered, in one of those ubiquitous pubs Ivo had enthused about on the ferry from Holland, but which, for some reason, they had never visited in Clitheroe.

Proceeding along Cheviot Street with the aim of locating such an establishment, he discovered that his surroundings were mainly residential. He passed a small park with a duck pond, shrubberies and children's swings, next to which was an elementary school where the young pupils were noisily enjoying midday break in the yard. He paused for a while to observe them, comforted by their innocent presence, noting that the boys mainly played a crude form of soccer, using chalked lines on the brick school walls to represent goalposts. The girls, by contrast, stood about in small groups, chatting to each other or to one of the adult supervisors. He formed the impression that he might soon grow to like living in such an area, despite evidence of its past prosperity and its evident signs of urban decay.

Cheviot Street issued in a major intersection, giving him a choice of direction. After waiting for a pedestrian signal at the traffic lights, he made a right turn onto Longsight Road, since straight ahead seemed to lead into another mainly residential area. Eventually, after passing rows of shops, he espied a painted sign hanging above an open doorway, an unmistakable smell of ale wafting out into the street. Ivo had told him to look out for such signs, each of which carried a distinctive name. He read 'The White Hart', beneath which was a depiction of a deer's head. This must be one of the celebrated pubs, he decided, entering gingerly and occupying a high stool facing the bar. His surroundings intrigued him. Along the bar were colorful beer pumps, each bearing an individual brand name, and on the wall behind the serving area were cabinets holding spirits, liqueurs and wines. A buxom woman wearing a dark-green apron, having finished drawing a pint of ale for another customer, approached him with a friendly smile.

"What will it be, luv?" she asked, breezily.

"Beer," he replied, rather hesitantly.

"Which kind?"

Zivko pointed to the pump nearest to him.

"Robinson's Bitter?" she asked. "Pint or half?"

Since her new customer merely looked puzzled, she held up glasses of different size. Zivko indicated the larger one. The landlady promptly drew him a pint measure.

"That all, luv?" she asked, passing it to him.

"Eat," he said.

The woman gave him a curious look as she handed him the menu, as if thinking 'not another immigrant'. The young Serb perused it carefully, but the various items meant little to him at first, until he saw the word 'steak'. He pointed to it.

"The steak sandwich, with salad?" she enquired.

The pub novice nodded.

"That will be nine pounds total," she said.

Zivko drew out the wad of banknotes Ivo had given him and peeled off a ten-pound bill. The landlady took it and returned a pound coin in change, before momentarily leaving the bar to pass the order to the chef. The initiate sipped his ale tentatively. It had a bitterer tang than the lagers he was familiar with back home and in Holland, but he thought he quite liked it, though it might take some getting used to. While awaiting his meal, he glanced round the room. Couples or small groups occupied the tables, eating and drinking; conversation was quite animated. High up in the far corner was a television set, tuned to a sports channel. When his meal arrived, Zivko transferred to a vacant table to get a better view of the screen, pleased to note that a live soccer match was about to start. He was still there two hours later, lingering over his second pint of Robinson's Bitter, trying to make it last. The lunch-hour trade had subsided and, as the bar lounge was now quieter, he could catch snatches of the live commentary. He understood enough to know that Oldham Athletic had just beaten Cardiff City by two goals to one.

It was just turned four o'clock when he arrived back at 93 Cheviot Street. He approached the front door and rang the bell. There was no answer. After a few moments, he rang again and stepped back to glance up at the windows. The faded lace curtain at a second-floor window moved slightly and he caught the fleeting image of a face, hoping it was Anna's. Shortly afterwards, he heard the sound of footfalls approaching the door. It opened barely a few inches and a face peered out.

"I come see Anna," he announced, in his broken English.

The door opened wider, to reveal a young woman wearing only a pink bathrobe. She pulled it tighter round her as she appraised the young man.

"Anna?" she asked, in surprise.

Zivko nodded.

"She is not here."

"She at hospital?"

The woman merely shrugged, implying that she had no idea of Anna's whereabouts, and shut the door in his face. Zivko Plesijc was non-plussed. He pressed the doorbell once again, but received no reply. Fighting back feelings of hurt and bewilderment, he was unsure what to do, or where to spend the night. Retracing his steps down Longsight Road towards The White Hart, the question was soon resolved. He noticed a Bed & Breakfast sign outside a brightly-painted building with attractive window boxes. He entered and booked in, surprised to find that it would cost only thirty-five pounds, breakfast included. Relaxing for a few minutes on the well-sprung mattress, to rest his feet after a deal of legwork, he then consulted Yellow Pages for the addresses of local hospitals, figuring that Anna must be employed at one of them. Making notes, he then went down to the residents lounge, which offered use of a computer, bringing up an Internet map of the city. After an hour or so of study, he had determined the precise location of several hospitals, as well as their approximate distance from his present whereabouts. He would set out early the following day, to visit each in turn, not feeling confident enough of his English to make telephone enquiries in advance.

◆   ◆   ◆

First thing Monday morning, after a welcome weekend break on his return from Basel, George Mason was summoned to the Chief Inspector's office.

"Had a worthwhile trip?" Harrington asked. He was in a buoyant mood, having spent the weekend visiting Glen Garioch distillery at Old Meldrum, near Aberdeen.

"Rather," came the unequivocal reply.

"So what do you have to report? Did you place a notice in the newspaper, as I suggested?"

"I did indeed, Chief Inspector," Mason replied. "After sorting through the replies, most of which were routine expressions of sympathy, I interviewed two people. One of them, by a stroke of luck, turned out to be Seifert's former mistress, Freni Kusnacht."

"Was she forthcoming?"

"Very much so. She told me several things of interest. Heini Seifert apparently moved to this country because he had been receiving death threats post-marked from Dresden."

"Why Dresden, in particular?"

"While awaiting replies to the newspaper notice," George Mason explained, "I called on my old friend Leutnant Kubler at Zurich. He suggested that I visit the Immigration Bureau at Bern, to ascertain the date of Seifert's entry into Switzerland as a permanent resident."

"And?" Harrington asked, expectantly.

"I discovered that Heini Seifert and Heinrich Feldman were one and the same person!"

"You don't say so, Inspector!" came his superior's surprised reaction. "You mentioned a Feldman at our last meeting, implying he had been an informer for the secret police."

"In which case," Mason reminded him, "he would have made quite a few enemies."

"People with scores to settle, presumably, after the collapse of the Communist regime?"

"Exactly."

"What else did this Freni Kusnacht have to say?"

"Among other things, that Seifert continued in medical practice, by opening a clinic at Clitheroe, just a few miles from Whalley. Also, that he had an estranged daughter whose name she did not recall, as well as a son Manfred, who died in a motoring accident."

"Do you have the address of the clinic?" an impressed Bill Harrington asked.

"Fortunately, Ms. Kusnacht maintained contact with her

former lover, to the extent of exchanging Christmas greetings. She mailed hers to Wellman Clinic, Clitheroe, Lancs."

"Then you had better be on your way up north again, Inspector. This is the first genuinely useful lead you have obtained."

"Am I to take Detective Sergeant Aubrey along?" Mason asked.

"I'll see if she's free of commitments," the other replied, "She was switched, temporarily, to a different case, at the behest of the Superintendent."

At that point, the desk phone rang, occupying the Chief Inspector in a conversation lasting several minutes. George Mason drained his tepid coffee and waited patiently for him to finish, gathering that the Superintendent was complaining about expense overruns. For his part, he was secretly hoping that Alison Aubrey would be re-assigned to the case.

"You mentioned another person of interest whom you met in Basel," Bill Harrington prompted, on replacing the receiver.

"Maurice Behrens," Mason replied. "He's the manager of Bank Linus Vogelin, a private investment bank of the type used by the wealthy to shield income from the various tax authorities, including our own Inland Revenue."

"And what did he have to say?"

"Very little of substance. He was as cagey as they come, but I did form the impression that Seifert held significant sums on account there. The minimum balance is a mere 500,000 francs."

Bill Harrington reacted in mock amazement.

"More than you or I could put together in two working life-times, eh, Inspector?"

"You bet, Chief Inspector."

"Proceeds of his clinical practice at Clitheroe, presumably?" the other then asked.

"Assuming that was his main source of income, yes."

"How soon can you get up there, Inspector, with a warrant to go over the books? You may also turn up bank statements, bank transfers and such-like. It might take you a little nearer discovering who wanted to kill him, but if the assassin was working out of Dresden, where you say he made enemies, I doubt that the Superintendent would be willing to allocate the resources necessary for what could prove a long-drawn-out investigation."

Mason's heart sank a little on hearing that. He had already put so much time and effort into cracking this case that it would go against the grain to assign it to the unsolved crimes file.

"I should be free by Wednesday, Chief Inspector," Mason assured him, "after tying up some loose ends here."

◆   ◆   ◆

Around noon on Wednesday, George Mason and Alison Aubrey re-appeared in Whalley, after taking an early express from London to Manchester, where they switched to the local service. They went directly to the police station to meet up with Sergeant Roy Wheeldon, whom they had telephoned in advance so that he could ascertain the precise location of Wellman Clinic, informing him of the link with Dr. Seifert. Within minutes, they were on the weaving country road to Clitheroe, following the same route in reverse as that taken by Ivo Grigorev and the young Serb. Sergeant Wheeldon was at the helm, pointing out Pendle Hill on the way. As they reached their destination, they were immediately struck by the absence of vehicles in the parking lot.

"Is this some sort of local holiday?" a bemused George Mason asked.

"Not that I am aware of," an equally puzzled Roy Wheeldon replied. "But it could be their lunch-hour."

The trio climbed out of the car and approached the main entrance, only to find the glass-paneled door locked. George Mason rang the bell, while his local colleague peered through the ground-floor windows front and back.

"No sign of life," Wheeldon said, "anywhere in this building."

"I don't think there has been anyone here for several days," Alison Aubrey remarked.

"What makes you say that?" her colleague asked.

"There's an accumulation of mail on the floor of the entrance hall," she pointed out. "You can just make it out through the dimpled glass."

The detective put his face close to the door and peered inside.

"By Jove, you're right, Alison," he said. "And newspapers too, by the look of it. Seems like they left in a hurry and forgot to cancel deliveries."

The police trio stood back and glanced up at the higher windows, in the off-chance of spotting some movement.

"What led you to link this place with the deceased?" an intrigued Roy Wheeldon asked.

"Remarkably enough," the Scotland Yard man replied, "I got the connection through a notice I placed in a Swiss newspaper. Seifert's former lover in Basel, a certain Freni Kusnacht, told me that she mailed Christmas greetings to this address. You were surely aware of the clinic's existence yourself, Sergeant?"

"It has a good reputation in this area," Wheeldon replied, "for treating certain types of men's health problems. But to my knowledge they never advertised their services, either in local newspapers or on television. I had the impression that it was one of those discreet private clinics relying mainly on a well-heeled clientele. I never came in contact with any of the medical personnel."

"No problems with the law?" Alison prompted.

The local officer shook his head vigorously.

"None whatsoever," he assured her.

"The question now," Mason said, "is how best to proceed, so that we can make a thorough search of the premises."

"You have a warrant?"

"Of course," Mason replied.

"Then we shall have to force an entry," Roy Wheeldon said, "which will take a little time. There's a locksmith I know of in

Clitheroe, someone we have used before. Why don't you and your young colleague in the meantime visit the pub across the way, The Cross Keys, have a bite to eat after your long journey and meet me back here in, say, forty-five minutes?"

The Scotland Yard pair exchanged approving glances.

"I just love these north-country pubs," Alison said. "Why don't we do just that, George? Besides, I'm really quite peckish."

Her senior colleague, ever amenable to downing a pint of real ale, acceded without demur. They made to cross the narrow road, as Sergeant Wheeldon climbed back into his car to cover the short distance to the center of town.

"What do you hope to discover at Wellman Clinic?" Alison asked, as they sat facing each other over beer and a plowman's lunch of Cheddar cheese, pickles and rye bread.

"Mainly personal records and names of contacts," Mason replied. "Bill Harrington and I think Seifert's death could have resulted from events in his past life in East Germany. I mentioned on the train about Seifert's links to the Stasi under his *alter ego*, Heinrich Feldman. If he received threatening letters in Basel, I should be very interested to discover if similar were sent to Wellman Clinic."

"But would you ever know who sent them, if they originated abroad?"

"That could involve a long enquiry, Alison. According to Bill Harrington, the Superintendant may not wish to expend too many resources on it. We'll keep our fingers crossed and hope for an early breakthrough. At least, we now know a deal more about the victim than we did two weeks ago."

"You'll crack the case, all right, George," Alison said, encouragingly. "I have every confidence in you."

The senior detective returned an ironic smile, hoping that her ready confidence would be justified. Within the allotted time, they finished their lunch and re-crossed the road to meet Sergeant Wheeldon, finding that the local locksmith had already effected entry. The interior of the premises looked as if it had been closed short-term, as for a weekend or public holiday. No attempt had been made to store away medical equipment, or to file documents in the small office at the rear; the kitchen still had dishes in the drying rack. George Mason opened the appointments book and quickly perused its contents; while Alison Aubrey mounted the stairs to vet the main living quarters. Sergeant Roy Wheeldon examined a folder containing what appeared to be sundry financial documents.

"Seems fairly routine stuff to me," Mason remarked. "As you said earlier, Sergeant, they specialized in men's health problems. There are recent appointments logged here for vasectomies, incontinence, prostatitis and erectile dysfunction. Charges vary, on a scale from sixty to three hundred pounds."

"That does not tally with the bank records, Inspector," Roy Wheeldon said, showing Mason a sheaf of statements from Bank Linus Vogelin. "These show deposits of a hundred thousand pounds, recorded monthly in the name of Dr. Heini Seifert."

"How far do those records go back?" Mason asked, a gleam of triumph in his eye.

"Almost two years," Wheeldon replied, after a quick check.

"That would be over two million pounds in total," Mason said. "No wonder the guy used a private Swiss bank. Have you also come across British bank statements showing transfers?"

"Only a bunch of dockets from Western Union," came the reply. "It seems he sent the money directly to Switzerland."

"To avoid Inland Revenue," Mason opined.

At that point, Alison Aubrey rejoined them, bursting with news.

"Three people were living here until very recently!" she announced. "One of them was female. A couple used the master bedroom, and a single male occupied the spare, leaving behind a girlie magazine and an empty packet of Dutch cigarettes."

"Have they left any belongings here?" her colleague asked.

"Very little," Alison replied. "The wardrobes and drawers have been cleared, apart from toiletry items including an empty perfume bottle, remnants of face powder and a dark lipstick. In the bathroom there are used tubes of toothpaste, a worn toothbrush and discarded razor cartridges. My guess is that the occupants of these premises, whoever they were, have left for good."

"Which presents us with a very interesting scenario, Alison," George Mason commented. "The way I read it is that they were probably assistants to Dr. Seifert. With the surgeon gone, they really had no other option to closing this place down."

"Suggesting that they must somehow have learned of his death," Alison said.

Her colleague pondered the implications of that remark for a few moments, before saying:

"That might very well be the case. The question is how they came by that knowledge, since it was withheld from the media."

"Perhaps they were complicit in the crime?" Roy Wheeldon put in.

"That is also a possibility," Mason agreed, reluctantly, since it would inevitably widen his field of enquiry.

"Any success in the office, George?" Alison then asked.

"We found Swiss bank statements showing transfers of large sums of money. There has definitely been a lot more going on here than routine male health procedures."

Alison Aubrey examined the documents, while Roy Wheeldon scanned the few remaining items in the financial folder.

"I see what you mean," she remarked, impressed at the sums involved.

"This looks like some sort of rental agreement," the local officer said, handing Mason a document headed Calder Valley Estates.

George Mason scanned it quickly.

"The rental agreement expires at the end of this month," he said, "but presumably it could have been renewed."

"Not likely to be, in the circumstances," Alison quipped.

"You had better contact the property owners, Sergeant," Mason advised, "and bring them up to date. They'll probably want to re-let."

"I can certainly do that, Inspector," Roy Wheeldon said. "And I could also take the appointments book, listing names of patients and their telephone numbers, to make routine checks."

"That would be very helpful, Sergeant," Mason said, as the trio headed towards the door. "You can always contact me at the Yard, if you come up with anything useful. Meanwhile, I'll take charge of the financial folder. Chief Inspector Harrington will be expecting something more concrete than theorizing, at this stage."

"Before I forget," Alison then said, producing a dark-green document and handing it to her colleague. "This looks like Dr. Seifert's passport. It was in a small bureau at the foot of the stairs."

"The photograph may prove useful," George Mason remarked, handing it to Sergeant Wheeldon after a brief inspection. "Why don't you take this too, to see if anyone recognizes it."

"Say, at The Three Fishes restaurant?" Wheeldon asked.

"Why not?"

Chapter Seven

Zivko Plesijc had spent the last two days walking the streets of Manchester. Unfamiliar with the English custom of driving on the left-hand side of the road, he had narrowly avoided being hit by speeding cars on at least two occasions, as he made to cross the road. With the aid of a rough map he had copied from the Internet, he had in turn visited the University Hospital, The Northern Eye Hospital, the Children's Hospital, the Dental Hospital and the Maternity Clinic. None of them had any knowledge of an Anna Nikolic. The best information he was able to gain, using his halting English, was from the head nurse at the Children's Hospital, the only person who seemed sympathetic to his plight. She interrupted her busy schedule to explain that, as a result of government cutbacks, many hospital staffs had been down-sized, some employees being laid off completely, others being reassigned to various parts of the country, particularly to some underserved rural areas.

That information, gleaned near the end of his second day exploring the bustling city, was of small comfort to the young Serb. If Anna had been transferred to a hospital elsewhere, he despaired of discovering its location. If she had been laid off and had obtained a different line of work, he felt sure that she would have remained at the Cheviot Street address to await his arrival. A third possibility, the most unattractive, was that she had lost her job altogether, given up on England and returned to Belgrade. Each evening, he had revisited the Longsight address in the hope of receiving a message from her via one of the current residents, whom she might have telephoned, aware that he would turn up at some point enquiring after her.

In growing despondency, he returned to the Bed & Breakfast each evening, rested for a while on the narrow bed and watched television to improve his English. After a while, he would take a shower, dress and walk the short distance to The White Hart. The lounge bar had become a sort of second home to him. It started to fill up with locals soon after seven o'clock and remained open until eleven. The regular patrons, who from their attire struck him as ordinary working people, played darts and dominoes, watched television, or just chatted among themselves. Some of them, with the goodwill and innate sociability of the northern English, tried to engage him in conversation and occasionally offered him a glass of beer. Zivko warmed to the friendliness of the pub atmosphere. It was just as Ivo had described it to him on the boat. He was content to watch a televised soccer match or a Hollywood film, while also taking sporadic interest in the intriguing games underway at nearby tables, to distract him from more pressing problems.

The chief of these, he recognized, as he made his way through steady rain to the pub on his final evening, was shortage of money. The amount Ivo had given him was rapidly being used up by accommodation, meals, tobacco and visits to the pub. Having economized on lunch by having just a feta cheese sandwich and a coffee at a small Greek restaurant near Albert Square, he was hungry by the time he reached the bar. The landlady greeted him in friendly fashion, drew him a pint of Robinson's Bitter and took his order for fish-and-chips. Zivko transferred with his beer to a corner table with an unrestricted view of the television set, looking forward to the generous portion of battered cod the chef would prepare, together with the most delicious golden-brown French fries he had ever eaten. Complimentary rolls and butter would complete a filling meal. There being no soccer match billed that evening on the sports channel – golf did not much appeal to him - he settled down to watch an old black-and-white Hitchcock movie, *Strangers on a Train*.

The lounge bar soon began to fill with regular patrons, relatively few of whom ordered food. Zivko gathered that they came mainly to socialize, having most likely taken their evening meal at home, in one of those small terraced houses along the narrow streets leading off the main thoroughfare. Groups of middle-aged men played dominoes, while the younger men monopolized the dart-board. Young couples were absorbed in their own affairs, paying little attention to their surroundings, causing the Serb a tinge of envy and sharpening his sense of disappointment at not meeting up with Anna. Small groups of women, perhaps neighbors or work colleagues, came in later, ordering shorts rather than beer and losing no time getting their heads together in earnest conversation. One of the younger women, an attractive blonde wearing what he considered rather florid make-up, glanced from time to time in his direction. Out of a natural shyness, but also on account of his absent girlfriend, he quickly averted his gaze, concentrating on the television.

Having eaten a satisfying meal and watched the movie through to its dramatic end, while also downing two pints of beer, he was still sitting at his corner table when the clock turned eleven and the last of the customers filed out. At that point, the lounge lights were dimmed and the pub staff arrived on the scene and began clearing the tables. The landlady, noting his after-hours presence, quickly approached him.

"Well, young man," she said, in mock-chiding tones, "have you no home to go to?"

"I have little money," he plaintively replied, calculating that this homely woman was someone he could confide in.

The landlady drew up a chair and sat facing him attentively, while her staff went about their final round of chores.

"And why is that, luv?" she asked, sympathetically.

"I looking for friend Anna, but not find."

"You should contact the police," she said at once, "if your girlfriend has gone missing."

At mention of the word 'police', a look of alarm spread across Zivko's features.

"No...no...no," he stammered. "No police."

His reaction confirmed what she had already half suspected, that she was dealing with an illegal immigrant. Having quite taken to his polite and unassuming manner over the past few days, that presented her with a predicament. It was her civic duty, she well knew, to report him to the authorities. But she could not bring herself to do that; the maternal instinct proved the stronger.

"Do you have somewhere to stay tonight?" she asked.

To her relief, Zivko nodded. Returning to the bar, she drew a twenty-pound note from the till, returned to his table and handed it to him. She had quickly decided on the best course to adopt, both to assist the needy young visitor and to relieve her of responsibility. After all, she reasoned, hadn't she a busy pub to run?

"Tomorrow morning," she said, "you must go directly to the Salvation Army and explain that you are penniless and trying to contact Anna. They will feed you and find you a bed until you can locate your friend. They may even help you do that."

"Salvation Army?" the young Serb enquired, with a puzzled look.

"They run a hostel right here in Longsight," she explained. "It's at the far end of Cheviot Street."

"I know Cheviot Street," he replied, feeling a little easier in his mind, especially since the woman's manner was reassuring.

"Now be off with you," she said, firmly. "It's against the law to remain here after closing time."

Zivko Plesijc, reacting more to her tone of voice than to

her actual words, which he only vaguely understood, gratefully pocketed the banknote, rose to his feet and left, emerging into the steady evening rain. To avoid a soaking, he hastened his steps towards his usual overnight accommodation. Feeling already a little drowsy from the quantity of ale he had drunk, he watched the late television news for a short while before clambering into bed and falling asleep, the image of the kindly landlady of The White Hart, alternating with that of Anna, before his nodding eyes.

The next day, after doing justice to a full English breakfast, he made his way as directed to the far end of Cheviot Street, casting a wistful glance at the windows of Number 93 as he passed by. Not entirely sure what to expect, he felt immediately reassured at the sight of uniformed personnel when he reached the Salvation Army hostel. They had their counterparts, quite similarly dressed, in his own country and, for all he knew, in many other countries too. A senior officer listened patiently to his story, took notes and asked him how to spell Anna's surname, Nikolic. He then led him into a large common-room where other inmates, male and female, were watching television, and enquired if he was hungry. Zivko Plesijc categorically shook his head; food was the least of his concerns at this point in time. As he entered and took a seat, several pairs of eyes briefly followed his movements, with studied indifference. Wasn't he just another down-and-out like themselves?

He had not been sitting there for more than half an hour, vainly trying to concentrate on the television program, before the same officer summoned him to an interview-room. On entering, his heart sank at the sight of two uniformed police officers, a man and a woman, sitting at a table facing a computer screen. The Salvation Army man withdrew, closing the door behind him.

"I am Sergeant Felstead," the male officer said, "and this is Constable Higgins."

The young woman smiled at him encouragingly, raising expectations in Zivko's mind that they had managed to locate Anna. But his hopes on that score were soon dashed.

"Name?" Sergeant Felstead asked.

"Zivko Plesijc."

"Can you spell that for me?"

The young Serb complied.

"Passport?" Constable Higgins then asked.

Zivko simply shrugged, causing the officer to look at him more sternly, before she said: "You are here illegally, aren't you?"

Zivko stared back at her, not understanding the term, or not wishing to.

"I don't think he knows much English," Felstead remarked to his colleague. "Try a different line."

"Where are you from?" Higgins asked.

"Belgrade."

"Serbia is not a member of the European Union," Felstead said to her. "Now he has real problems."

"Why have you come to England?" the constable asked.

"To find Anna," Zivko replied. "She working here. Nurse."

The two officers exchanged skeptical glances.

"Which hospital?" Higgins asked, dubiously.

The young man shook his head, looking helpless.

"He does not know," Felstead decided. "Maybe it's a cock-and-bull story he's making up to provide some sort of cover. More likely, he's an economic migrant who's somehow managed to slip through the system."

"Who brought you here?" Constable Higgins then asked.

Zivko weighed his options before answering, deciding that loyalty to Ivo was now misplaced. If the clinic had kept its part of the bargain and everything had gone according to plan, he would be a thousand pounds to the good. He would not be in this predicament now, since he would not have needed to contact the Salvation Army, who had evidently lost no time alerting the authorities. He could also have continued his search for Anna, without any clear idea of how he would do that. Now that he was unfortunate enough to find himself in the hands of the police, he decided to make a clean breast of things. Co-operation might somehow help his situation.

"I come with Ivo," he said, "from Delft."

"Ivo who?" he asked.

The young man shrugged.

"He doesn't know," Constable Higgins said.

"Wife name is Marika."

"Ivo and Marika," the sergeant said, sarcastically. "That really tells us a lot."

"Where did he take you?" the young constable asked.

"Wellman Clinic, Clitheroe," Zivko confidently replied. He had memorized the name from letter-heads he had seen.

"For what purpose?"

The young Serb merely looked blank, lacking the vocabulary to describe an abortive kidney transplant. The two officers exchanged puzzled glances, as Sergeant Felstead added as much relevant information as he could to his computer file.

"We'll contact Lancashire County Police," he then told his colleague. "Clitheroe is their province. They're best placed to check out his story." To Zivko, he said: "You're to come with us, young man. Grab your belongings and follow us outside."

With that, he shut down the computer and rose from his chair. Constable Higgins opened the door and Zivko, fearing that the chips were now well and truly down, reluctantly followed them out.

"Irlam Detention Center?" Higgins asked.

The sergeant nodded.

"Their interpreters will get the full story out of him," he said. "He seems inclined to co-operate, which may help his case a little in the long run. But my guess is that he will be deported."

"Do you think, Sergeant?" the constable asked, "that his girl-friend Anna may also be here illegally?"

"On balance, no," the other replied. "The National Health Service has in recent times hired nurses from abroad, especially from Eastern Europe, so she may well be here legitimately. In any case, Constable, it's not our priority to chase after illegal immigrants. We can safely leave that to the Home Office."

◆　　◆　　◆

The following day, as he was catching up on paperwork at his desk at Scotland Yard, George Mason received a call from Roy Wheeldon.

"Good morning, Inspector," the sergeant said. "How are things with you?"

"Middling," Mason replied. "How's yourself?"

"Can't complain, thank you. I did make routine checks on Wellman Clinic patients, as you suggested."

"Turn up anything?"

"Not in that direction," Wheeldon replied. "They all visited the clinic for routine procedures. But there has been a kind of breakthrough in the case."

George Mason sat bolt upright.

"Say that again," he said.

"There's been a breakthrough, of sorts. A Sergeant Clive Felstead, of Manchester City Police, rang Lancashire County Police to inform them that he had taken into custody an illegal immigrant, one Zivko Plesijc. It seems that Plesijc named Wellman Clinic in Clitheroe. Felstead wanted us to vet the place, but I told him we had already done so."

"That's a most interesting development," the detective said. "Plesijc could very well have been the occupant of the spare bedroom Alison Aubrey checked out."

"That's what I was thinking."

"So you've presumably got the names of the other two occupants?"

"Ivo and Marika," came the enthusiastic reply.

"Apart from telling me they're not British, Sergeant, that does not enlighten me a great deal. Surnames would be more helpful."

"All I can say in addition, Inspector, is that they are both from East Europe," Wheeldon said. "Zivko Plesijc himself is from Belgrade, but he couldn't explain what he was doing in Britain, aside from trying to locate his girlfriend, a nurse named Anna Nikolic."

"So you have no idea why he was at the clinic?"

"Irlam Detention Center is working on that, but they're having problems finding an interpreter who speaks his language."

"Which would be Serbo-Croat, I believe," the savvy detective said.

"I'll take your word for it, Inspector."

"It could be that he was there in connection with a Europe-wide kidney scam Bill Harrington mentioned a while back. The Home Office alerted him to it, but we dismissed it as unlikely, in view of our border controls."

"You may well be correct, Inspector," Roy Wheeldon replied.

"I'd stake half my pension on it," George Mason joked.

"Something else of interest came up," the other then said. "The Bangladeshi waiter at The Three Fishes in Great Mytton recognized the passport photo of Heini Seifert. He's pretty certain that's one of the customers who lunched there on April 11th last."

"That's also likely to prove useful," Mason said. "Now we have several pieces of this puzzle, if only we can fit them together."

"Anything else I can do at this end?" Roy Wheeldon enquired.

"You could go back to Wellman Clinic, Sergeant. But this time take a forensic expert with you, someone who may be able to tell from all that medical equipment left lying around if kidney transplants might have taken place. The bank transfers to Basel indicate high-value business, above and beyond routine medical practice. And now we also have this displaced young Serb to take into account."

"I'll do my best, Inspector," Wheeldon said, ringing off.

Chapter Eight

Rachel Slade slept late following her arrival the previous evening from England, appearing in the dining-room of Der Hirsch Hotel towards the end of breakfast service. Choosing a vacant table by the window, whence she could look out over an elevated cobbled square with a stone fountain playing, she lost no time ordering muesli with yoghurt, followed by poached eggs and coffee. There was now only a sprinkling of guests scattered about the large, paneled room, on whose walls she noted alpine motifs and a boar's head. Feeling pleased with her choice of accommodation, she glanced at the program for the trade fair to be held over the course of the next few days at Zunfthaus zur Schuhmachern, apparently the home of the Shoemakers Guild dating from the Middle Ages, which bordered the River Limmat. She would visit it first thing this morning, to view the latest trends in her specialized field and attend the presentation given by a prominent Italian designer on fashion and jewelry. Renzo Gambini was flying in from Rome that day, especially for the purpose. She was nursing vague hopes of a personal introduction to him.

After a rather hurried breakfast, she emerged into the bright

morning sunshine, heading down narrow flights of stone steps leading from the Altstadt to the river embankment, where she soon
located the storied guildhall. Once inside, she found the fair already
well under way, recalling that the Swiss generally started work an
hour earlier than the British; a glance at her wristwatch told her it
was almost ten o'clock. Many buyers were already in attendance,
most of whom she thought would be small business people like herself, together with representatives of up-market department stores
and leading fashion houses. As she mingled with the crowd, closely
examining the displays in turn and chatting with representatives,
she heard American, Chinese and Japanese voices too, confirming
her impression that the fair was a truly international affair, drawing
people from around the globe. She was not able, however, to effect a
personal introduction to the Italian celebrity, who was whisked off
into private meetings with the more important clients immediately
following his presentation. Shortly after two o'clock, having booked
several items for her own stock, she felt that she had seen enough
for one day and made her way outside. She would approach the fair
with a fresh perspective later in her stay.

Crossing Munsterhof, an elegant classical-style square, she soon
found herself on Bahnhofstrasse, which she had heard described
as Europe's most expensive street. A glance at window displays,
as she headed in the general direction of the lake, confirmed this
reputation. Goldsmiths, silversmiths, jewelers, art dealers, oriental
rug merchants and antiquarians were all represented. The price-
tags were unabashedly aimed at the very rich, whom she pictured
as bankers, fund managers, foreign residents including celebrities
enjoying the low tax regime, retired businessmen and nouveau riche
visitors from Russia and Asia. But she had not come to Zurich,
she told herself, on a high-end shopping expedition, preferring
to use her available funds for stock purchases. She did, however,
form an idea of the sort of things, especially original artwork and
hand-woven rugs, she might aspire to when she herself might be
counted among the wealthy. For the present, she was content with

brief visits to the gown shops and cosmeticians, before indulging her sweet tooth at one of the specialist chocolate boutiques she espied. Saving her purchase for later, she found a vacant table at one of the busy sidewalk cafes, ordered a bottle of Perrier and an open sandwich, while attempting to discern the different nationalities of the passers-by.

After her snack, she spent the remainder of the afternoon sitting in a small park facing the lake, to catch up on the trade brochures she had picked up at the fair, her attention from time to time distracted by strolling musicians and groups of small children with their nannies. From her seat, she could watch the lake steamers depart from the quay and the yachts tack across the shimmering surface of the lake. Her husband Craig had long wanted to own a yacht, she mused, even if sailing one would be restricted to local reservoirs; she hoped at some point to be able to help him achieve this goal. As she heard the clock-tower of the Peterkirche strike the hour of four, she reluctantly relinquished her lakeside seat and made her way back along Bahnhofstrasse towards her hotel. She would take a shower and change for the evening's champagne reception at the Zunfthaus, hoping that Renzo Gambini would also be present and perhaps circulate among the guests. Afterwards, she would enjoy a light supper at Der Hirsch and retire early in readiness for the busy day ahead.

✦   ✦   ✦

Next day, immediately after breakfast, she covered on foot the short distance from the Altstadt to the Hauptbahnhof, where she caught the 9.15 a.m. train to Basel, arriving there mid-morning. Following Maurice Behrens' directions, she soon located the premises of Bank Linus Vogelin just outside the station. He was expecting her by prior appointment made the previous day, soon after her arrival in Zurich. A smartly-clad receptionist showed her to his private office.

"*Guten Morgen*, Frau Slade," he said, proffering his hand.

"Good-day to you, Herr Behrens," his visitor confidently rejoined.

"Please do take a seat."

Rachel sat down, taking in at a glance the elegant furnishings and the vase of fresh flowers.

"Peonies," the banker said, noting her interest.

"They bloom earlier here than in England," she smilingly observed.

"Because we are significantly farther south," Behrens explained. "Now what is it you wish to see me about?"

"As I explained briefly on the telephone yesterday," Rachel replied, "I wish to release my father's assets held at this bank."

The banker shifted posture, to face his visitor directly.

"I must admit I was very surprised to learn from you of his untimely death," he said, disingenuously, not wishing to disclose prior knowledge of that event obtained from a certain visitor from Scotland Yard.

"It was sudden and unexpected," Rachel replied, momentarily casting her eyes downward.

"Please accept my sincere condolences, Frau Slade."

She attempted a half-smile, as she drew some documents from her shoulder-bag.

"This is a copy of my father's will," she said, passing it to him.

As the banker perused it closely, a look of some surprise crossed his tanned features.

"It names you as sole heir," he said, after several minutes, "*and* sole executor."

"That seems to surprise you," Rachel quickly noted. "Should it?"

Maurice Behrens, clearing his throat, tapped nervously with his finger-tips on the highly-polished table top.

"Forgive me, Frau Slade," he said, after an awkward pause, "but my understanding was that you and your father - God rest his soul – had long been estranged. That accounts for my surprise at sight of this will, which I note was drawn up only a month ago."

"There was a reconciliation," Rachel replied, matter-of-factly. "Recently."

The banker's astute features registered surprise.

"Would I be correct in thinking, Madame," he enquired, "that your estrangement from your father dated from around the time of your mother's death?"

It was his visitor's turn to look surprised.

"It isn't really any of your business," she tartly replied. "But that is in fact true, for what it is worth."

"Forgive my curiosity," Behrens apologized. "You see, I attended Dr. Seifert's trial and have long been curious about his children. I was aware, for example, that Manfred died in a motoring accident."

Rachel's eyes took on a sad cast at mention of her brother. She regarded her interlocutor closely, with a hint of warmer feelings, since he seemed in a way quite close to her family and concerned about their welfare.

"Manfred's death affected my mother deeply," she said. "I don't think she ever really recovered from it."

"What was your reaction to the trial verdict?" Behrens then ventured.

His visitor's face registered irritation at the blunt question. Averting her eyes towards the vase of peonies, she said:

"I have my personal views on that, Herr Behrens. I prefer to keep them that way."

"Of course, of course," flustered the banker. "Please forgive my curiosity. I did not mean to intrude on your privacy."

"Could we perhaps just attend to the business in hand?" Rachel Slade asked, abruptly changing the subject.

Maurice Behrens scanned the document again, before saying:

"Everything seems to me to be in order. Since your father's assets are held mainly in this country, rather than in England, I shall get our company lawyers to arrange probate. We can side-step the British courts."

"How long will it take?"

"Usually a matter of weeks, unless someone challenges the will."

"My father has no surviving relatives, apart from myself."

"Then probate would normally be quite straightforward," the banker said. "We shall also need a death certificate."

Rachel passed a second document to him, which he scrutinized carefully.

"Severe spinal trauma," he read, with a deep sigh. "The result of an accident?"

His visitor gravely nodded.

"My father suffered a fall while out hiking," she explained.

"Most unfortunate," the other remarked. "I knew him for a keen outdoors man. Last time he was here, he told me that he had recently done Nordic skiing in Bavaria and hiking in the English Lakes."

"He was very active," Rachel said, "up till the end."

"It would appear so, Madame. Leave this matter in our capable hands. We shall get in touch with you again in about a month's time. Are you staying by any chance in Basel?"

"In Zurich, actually, to attend the trade fair."

"That would be Costume Jewelry & Accessories, would it not?"

Rachel nodded.

"We received notice of it here," Behrens explained. "Some of our important clients are also attending."

"It's an annual event," Rachel said. "Very international."

"That is my understanding, Frau Slade. Now, is there anything else I can do for you, while you are here?"

"I take it I can count on your complete discretion and confidentiality regarding this matter?"

"Absolutely."

A well-pleased Rachel Slade, keen to get back to Zurich to re-visit the fair, rose to her feet and shook Behrens' hand. As she left, the banker pondered the delicate situation. The will seemed genuine enough; the death certificate was properly drawn up and signed by a physician, giving a cause of death consistent with Frau Slade's account. But how had this attractive young woman, his newly-reconciled daughter, learned of her father's death, he wondered? And how was it that her account differed markedly from Inspektor Mason's? The matter placed him in a dilemma. If he initiated probate in the Swiss courts with the current documents, he might very well obtain a wealthy new client, assuming he could persuade her to invest part of her substantial legacy with Linus Vogelin. Ordering fresh coffee from his receptionist, he decided to defer that decision until later, fully recognizing that he also had a duty under Swiss law to report any suspicion of criminality to the police.

+ + +

"Good to have you back on board, Alison," George Mason said to the young detective sergeant, as she joined him for a morning conference.

"So what's new in the Seifert case?" she enquired, facing him across his cluttered desk.

"I made a second visit to Switzerland," he replied. "Sorry you couldn't come along."

"I was put on a different case while you were gone, but that has now been handed to a rookie. Bill Harrington re-assigned me."

"You missed a good trip," Mason said. "My main discovery – would you believe it? - was that Heini Seifert and Heinrich Feldman were one and the same person."

Alison Aubrey reacted in amazement.

"How on earth did you find that out, George?" she asked.

"On a visit to the Immigration Bureau in Bern, I discovered that

Heinrich Feldman, in the course of applying for a Swiss residence permit, changed his name by deed poll to Heini Seifert."

"Why would he have done that?"

"My contact Leutnant Rudi Kubler, of Zurich Polizei Dienst, had a theory that former members of the Stasi, the East German secret police, made their way on reunification to neighboring countries, where they often changed their names."

"Because they feared reprisals for their activities under the Communist regime?" Alison shrewdly asked.

George Mason nodded.

"And we already discovered, didn't we in Dresden, that Feldman was a police informer?" he said.

"So you are thinking that Feldman, aka Seifert, was killed in revenge?"

"At this point, I'm only saying there's a plausible explanation for his move to Switzerland and his change of name."

"The implications are very interesting, to say the least," his assistant opined.

"No question of that."

"And did you also revisit Basel?"

"I certainly did," Mason replied. "I interviewed his former lover, Freni Kusnacht, who tipped us off about Wellman Clinic. She also told me that Seifert had an estranged daughter, and that the reason for the estrangement was her mother Celine's death."

"You mean that the daughter, contrary to the trial verdict, may have held her father responsible?"

"Quite possibly. Ms. Kusnacht, having also attended the trial, came to the same conclusion."

"That Seifert was guilty of murdering his wife?"

"Exactly."

"You've had a busy time, George," Alison conceded, "while I've been tied up on a routine case of shoplifting."

"It's all grist for the mill, Sergeant."

At that point, Alison Aubrey, to stretch her legs, rose from her chair and crossed to the window, looking down on the steady rain falling across Whitehall.

"Anything else to relate?" she enquired.

George Mason swung his swivel chair around to face her.

"I also found out that Dr. Seifert kept large sums of money on deposit there, at a private bank called Linus Vogelin."

"Any leads on their provenance?" Alison asked.

"The banker, Maurice Behrens, would tell me nothing on that score, invoking laws on Swiss banking secrecy. But I now have other sources."

"Which are?"

"Late yesterday afternoon, Sergeant Roy Wheeldon rang me from Whalley. It seems that the Manchester City Police apprehended an illegal immigrant, name of Zivko Plesijc, who speaks little English. He was taken to Irlam Detention Center, where he told officials through an interpreter that he was taken from Delft in Holland to Clitheroe, Lancashire, to barter one of his kidneys for a thousand pounds and entry into England, where he has a girlfriend named Anna Nikolic."

"And it would be Dr. Seifert who was scheduled to perform the operation?" Alison asked, the light of understanding dawning across her alert features.

"The like of which he had probably been doing for the last three years," Mason ruefully replied. "Hence the regular transfers of money to Basel."

"But Seifert wasn't there to remove Zivko's kidney?"

"For the simple reason that, by that time, he was dead, Alison. Plesijc claims he was given two hundred pounds living expenses by a Romanian named Ivo, who also worked at the clinic, and dropped off by car in the Longsight area of Manchester."

"Where his friend Anna supposedly lived?"

"Except that she had moved on by the time he arrived – hence his approach to the Salvation Army, who shopped him straight away."

"Poor guy," Alison said, sympathetically. "So where is this Anna?"

"The police have traced her to a hospital in Leeds. She is quite legitimate, having been recruited to the National Health Service through official channels."

"What about Wellman Clinic?"

"Ivo and his wife Marika, who were based there until shortly before we called there with Sergeant Wheeldon, have presumably fled, to avoid arrest. They could be anywhere right now. My guess would be the South of France."

"Not our concern, George. We only have to find a murderer."

"You can say that again, Alison."

◆　　◆　　◆

Marika Grigorev woke early that morning, made coffee and attempted to rouse her husband, who was sleeping heavily after a late night at one of Rotterdam's leading restaurants, where they had been celebrating their wedding anniversary. Half an hour later, a rather bleary-eyed Ivo joined her in the diner-kitchen of their luxury apartment and poured himself a mug of fresh Java. Marika then set about preparing a simple meal of cereals and eggs Benedict, keeping half an eye on the television screen to monitor the latest news. One item in particular caught her attention.

"Did you hear that, Ivo?" she asked, concernedly.

Her still drowsy husband merely grunted.

"It says on the news that a prominent surgeon has been arrested for performing illegal organ transplants."

"Where would that be?" came the half-hearted response.

"Somewhere in Albania. I didn't catch the name of the place."

"Did it mention the Omega Network?" a suddenly more alert Ivo asked, sitting up in his chair.

"I didn't hear that. It mentioned the owner of the clinic, the surgeon, ancillary medical staff and a health ministry official as all being involved."

"I doubt it will affect our operation," Ivo said, rising from his chair and pacing the room thoughtfully. "Probably some rival outfit."

"I do hope you're right, Ivo," Marika said, laying the simple meal on the table.

As they moments later sat down to breakfast, he said:

"The black market takes many forms, Marika. In some places, prisoners have been executed for the express purpose of harvesting their organs. Elsewhere, needy people lured with promises of financial gain have received not so much as a sou for their trouble. At least, we have been able to provide a legitimate service."

"Like smuggling people into the United Kingdom and helping them find employment in the black economy? Plus compensation of one thousand pounds per kidney?"

As his hangover began to abate, Ivo Grigorev tackled his meal with growing appetite, requesting more toast, while thinking up a suitable response to his wife's uncharacteristically critical comment. Hadn't she too prospered from their association with Dr. Seifert?

"Unlike many in this business, we have not callously exploited people," he gave as his considered reply. "My conscience is clear on that. Our donors knew exactly what they were entering into, and we have always kept our part of the bargain. If we have broken a few laws in the process, and fallen foul of Immigration, those are relatively minor matters."

Marika smiled to herself at his ability to gloss over the ethical considerations. As a trained nurse, she had few doubts that they too were exploiting people, especially by paying them a small fraction of the value of their organs. She salved her own conscience with the thought that such matters had been the concern of her husband and Dr. Seifert; she herself was a small cog in the wheel, whose main role concerned the domestic arrangements at the clinic, together with minimal nursing duties. Transferring used dishes to the sink, she fell to wondering what had become of their latest donor, Zivko Plesijc; whether he had in fact met up with his girlfriend Anna.

"What time is your appointment with Fedor?" she then asked, seeing that her husband was now fully alert.

"Nine o'clock, at the café across the way."

"It's turned eight already," Marika said. "You'll just have time to finish your food, shower and get dressed."

Ivo Grigorev quickly finished eating and crossed briefly to the balcony to get some fresh air, before heading to the bathroom. With only minutes to spare, he emerged from the apartment building in casual attire, lit a small Dutch cigar and crossed the quiet residential street to sit at his favorite café table beneath the chestnut trees, now in full blossom. Minutes later, a slim individual in a sharp gray suit and sporting dark glasses, joined him. They ordered black coffee with aquavit.

"You left England in rather a hurry, I believe?" Fedor ironically remarked.

Ivo merely nodded.

"What was the problem?"

"Dr. Seifert's daughter showed up one day, saying that her father had died of a broken neck suffered in a fall while out hiking. Marika and I were stunned by the news. In the absence of the surgeon, we had no option but to close down the facility and cancel appointments."

"That's terrible news, Ivo," Fedor said. "He will be difficult to replace."

"It will mean opening a new center elsewhere in Britain."

"Eventually, that may be on the cards, if we can find a replacement to do the surgery. New premises should not be too difficult to set up, perhaps in the remote south-west of the country. Our activities can easily be disguised in a men's health facility."

"I'll leave that in your capable hands, Fedor," Ivo Grigorev said.

"What about the new donor, Zivko Plesijc?" the other then asked.

"We couldn't, of course, pay him the usual fee," Ivo replied. "I gave him expenses money and dropped him off at his girlfriend's place in Manchester. I assume she took him in hand."

"Is he reliable?"

"Absolutely. His main aim in this venture, as it has been with most of the donors on my route, was to effect entry into Britain. That much he has now achieved."

"You will, all the same, have to lie low for a while, until we can find a replacement for Dr. Seifert. Is there any way you could be traced back here to Rotterdam?"

"None whatsoever," Ivo confidently asserted. "None of my donors knew of my current address. I met all of them in different parts of Holland and Belgium, as you yourself know, having selected and vetted them."

"There will be problems in the supply chain," Fedor then said. "Some of our people have been arrested in Tirane. We shall have to suspend operations for a while."

"There was something about that on the news this morning," a perturbed Ivo Grigorev said. "Marika and I felt sure it could not involve our network."

"Omega is a Europe-wide organization, with many ramifications," the other said, chasing the aquavit with the coffee and lighting a filter cigarette. "We rely on the goodwill and discretion of a large number of people. Someone has obviously betrayed that trust."

"A disgruntled donor, perhaps?" Ivo ironically asked.

"How any given branch of Omega operates is their concern," Fedor impatiently replied. "Our top men have enough on their hands bribing health ministry officials to turn a blind eye to dubious activities at clinics and hospitals in their province. We could hardly function without their cooperation."

"Wellman Clinic was regularly given a clean bill by Health Ministry inspectors," Ivo said.

"A case in point, Ivo. But if we re-start our operation in a different part of Britain, we shall have to prepare the groundwork anew and identify fresh ministry officials to approach. What are your immediate plans?"

"Marika and I are leaving for a fortnight's holiday on the Dalmatian Coast, preceded by a short visit to her family in Bucharest."

"An excellent idea," Fedor said. "Things may well have settled down again by the time you return. Once the Tirane trial is over, we shall cut our losses and concentrate on new markets. The Middle East is beginning to look promising."

"I feel sure we shall rebound," Ivo said. "The demand for kidney transplants will hardly dry up."

"Unless stem cell research comes up with a viable means of organ regeneration," his contact countered.

"Some distance into the future, my good friend," Ivo Grigorev confidently asserted.

"We shall see," the other replied, more circumspectly. "My regards to Marika, and bon voyage!"

Chapter Nine

Back at the office on Monday morning, after a much-needed weekend break, George Mason was surprised to receive a phone call from Maurice Behrens, who rang shortly after the detective's routine conference with Bill Harrington.

"*Guten Morgen*, Inspektor Mason," he began. "How are things with you today?"

"Can't complain," Mason replied. "How's yourself?"

"Good," Behrens buoyantly rejoined.

"What can I do for you, Herr Behrens?"

The banker's conscience, after weighing civic duty against commercial profit, had gained the upper hand.

"You asked me to inform you," he continued, "about any movement on the Seifert account."

"I did indeed, Herr Behrens."

"A few days ago, I was approached by Dr. Seifert's daughter who, much to my surprise, showed me a valid will. I see no alternative but to put the deceased's estate through probate in the Swiss courts. Our company lawyers already have the matter in hand."

It took several moments for the significance of these remarks to sink in.

"This is interesting news," Mason said, eventually. "I was aware that Seifert had a daughter, from whom I believe he had become estranged. But I did not know her name."

"Rachel Slade," Behrens informed him. "I too was under the impression that they had not spoken in years, probably as a result of her mother Celine's death. But Frau Slade claims there had been a reconciliation. Quite recently, too."

"She stood to gain by her father's death?" the detective pointedly asked.

"She is, as a matter of fact, the sole beneficiary of his estate."

George Mason whistled aloud, drawing the attention of Alison Aubrey, who entered from the adjoining office.

"No doubt you have her current address and telephone number?" he said.

"That I do not have, unfortunately, Herr Inspektor. She is going to contact me in about a month's time, assuming there are no legal challenges to the will."

"There could be any number of Rachel Slades living in England," a slightly deflated George Mason said. "What else could you tell me about her?"

"She was in Zurich recently, I do know that. Attending a jewelry trade fair."

George Mason, giving Alison Aubrey a friendly nod, perked up considerably.

"If that is the case, she will probably be in the jewelry trade herself. We shall look into it closely. Now what about a death certificate? I assume there is one."

"Frau Slade showed it to me," the banker replied. "I have a copy of it in front of me now."

"Cause of death?" Mason asked.

"Severe spinal trauma."

"In other words, a broken neck, much as I would have figured. Can you tell me, Herr Behrens, who signed the certificate?"

"Dr. Ivo Grigorev, of Wellman Clinic, Clitheroe."

The detective was beside himself with excitement.

"Get this, Alison," he said, in an aside, "Seifert's death certificate was issued by Wellman Clinic!"

"Is everything all right, Inspektor?" the concerned banker asked, overhearing his remark.

"Just bringing my assistant, Detective Sergeant Aubrey, up to date," Mason replied.

"Is there anything else you need to know?"

"For the time being, no. But I reserve the privilege of contacting you again, should the need arise. You have been most helpful, Herr Behrens, and I thank you for it."

"My pleasure," the other said, ringing off.

George Mason rose from his chair to greet his assistant, whose look conveyed keen anticipation.

"A breakthrough, George?" she asked.

"You can say that again, Alison! We now have a prime suspect, in the person of Dr. Seifert's own daughter, Rachel Slade!"

"This is really great news," the young sergeant said. "My congratulations, George!"

"All credit to you too, Alison, for your by no means inconsiderable contribution."

Alison, momentarily basking in her superior officer's approval, soon returned a quizzical smile.

"One thing puzzles me," she said. "How did Seifert actually die? Did he suffer a fall on Whalley Nab? Was he pushed? Or was he attacked at the foot of the drop?"

"What makes you ask that?"

"The single cuff-link found near the body would seem to indicate a struggle. Would a young woman such as Rachel Slade be capable of breaking someone's neck?"

"I take your point, Alison," George Mason replied. "The

monogram on the cuff-link does not refer to either Heini Seifert or to Heinrich Feldman, who were in fact one and the same person, as we have already established."

"Therefore," the younger officer said, "there must have been another person at the scene. The question now is who?"

Mason glanced approvingly in Alison's direction, appreciating her acumen.

"At least, we're on the right track," he said, after a while, "even if we don't yet have all the answers."

"Our next step?"

"I should like you to go over to Westminster Public Library and see if you can find a directory of the jewelry trade. They keep all sorts of reference books like that. Look for the name Rachel Slade. If entries are broken down into specific regions, try the Northwest first, then Yorkshire, before trying elsewhere."

"I can certainly do that for you, George," Alison said. "Soon as I've checked my mail, I'll get over there and report back."

As she left his office, George Mason made his second visit that morning to Bill Harrington's office. The Chief Inspector, who was just pouring himself a tot of his current favorite in malt whiskeys, the Glen Garioch, glanced up in some surprise.

"Problems, Inspector?" he enquired.

"On the contrary!" the other exclaimed. "We now have some solutions, including the name of a prime suspect in the Seifert case – his daughter, Rachel Slade."

"You don't say so!" Harrington said, rising to his feet.

"And that is not all," George Mason continued. "We now have the full name of the medic known as Ivo, who was based at Wellman Clinic, which we suspect of performing illegal kidney transplants."

"Go on," Harrington urged.

"Dr. Ivo Grigorev, who I believe is of Serbian nationality, working partly out of Holland. I believe his role was to get the donors illegally into Britain."

"A great start to a new week, Inspector," his superior said. "My compliments. It's as the Home Office suspected. The black market in human organs has, inevitably, reached our own shores."

"Alison Aubrey is doing some further research at Westminster Library, before we can make our next move."

"And I'll contact the Dutch police, regarding Grigorev," Harrington promised. "Kommandant Klaas Hendrijks will be delighted at this development."

◆　　◆　　◆

Two days later, George Mason and Alison Aubrey took the 8.45 a.m. inter-city train from London to Preston, where they transferred to the local service for Blackpool. On arrival at the storied resort town, they walked along the promenade in the direction of Talbot Square, the address given for Rachel Slade's boutique in *Jewelry & Related Trades Directory*, which Alison had consulted. The tide was out and the legendary Golden Mile of sandy beach was dotted with early-season trippers, family groups with children making sandcastles, teenagers playing ball games and immigrants who seemed to Mason a trifle overdressed for a day at the seaside.

"Interesting place," Alison remarked, as they neared North Pier. "I've heard a lot about it, of course, but never actually been here before today."

"Playground of the North, they used to call it," her colleague opined.

"That was before the motor car, air travel and package tours, I expect," Alison said.

"Exactly," Mason replied. "It was the preferred destination for industrial workers on their annual week's holiday. They called it Wakes Week, for some reason."

"Nowadays, people are just as likely to visit Thailand, I imagine, as the British coast."

"Modern affluence," her colleague replied. "But resorts such as this seem to hold their own, all the same. Day-trippers, who probably account for most of the people you see here today; weekenders; conference attendees. You name it."

"Very popular with political parties, too," Alison said, "for their annual jamborees."

On reaching the pier, they crossed over the tramway leading to Fleetwood, a fishing port a few miles farther north that doubled as a vacation resort, and waited for a pedestrian signal to cross the main road. They then found themselves in Talbot Square, where they quickly located the jewelry boutique. A young woman, seeing in them two welcome customers on what had so far been a quiet day, greeted them in friendly fashion as they entered.

"We have some new lines," she said, optimistically, "direct from the Zurich trade fair."

"Mrs. Rachel Slade?" George Mason queried.

The serious look on his face immediately cramped her style.

"Yes?" she replied, uncertainly.

"I am Inspector Mason from Scotland Yard, and this is my colleague Detective Sergeant Aubrey," he said, producing ID. "We wish to interview you in connection with the death of your father, Dr. Heini Seifert."

The young jeweler's face paled, but her eyes feigned indignation.

"I do not know what you are referring to," she said.

"Is there somewhere we can talk more privately?" Alison Aubrey asked.

"If you insist," she replied, locking the shop door and leading them through to a small office at the rear of the building.

"Your father, Dr. Seifert, was found dead of a broken neck at the foot of Whalley Nab, on April 12th last," Mason said.

"That is news to me," Rachel replied. "My father and I have not been in contact for several years. It's a shock to me to learn of his death."

"Not so great a shock as to prevent you filing his will at Bank Linus Vogelin in Basel," the detective said.

Rachel's eyes narrowed, but she made no comment.

"Where were you on April 11th last?" Alison Aubrey asked.

"I think," Rachel replied, "that was the day I had lunch with my uncle."

"Lunch with uncle," Mason repeated, noting it down. "Where would that be?"

"In Longridge," came the reply. "At the…er…The Pendle Inn."

"Your uncle's name?"

"Ralph Miller."

"His current address?"

"The Gables, Goosenargh."

"He would be your mother's brother?"

Rachel's eyes opened wide in surprise.

"How could you possibly know something like that?" she asked.

"We know quite a lot about you and your family," Alison said.

"Your mother died of a drug overdose at Basel," George Mason added.

"That is tragically true," the young woman replied. "I have never really recovered from her death. She is ever in my thoughts."

"Did you blame your father?" Mason pointedly asked.

The blunt question stunned her for a moment.

"I have my own views on what caused mother's death," she replied, icily. "You should read the transcript of the ensuing trial if you want more information."

"I have already done so," the detective said.

Rachel again reacted in surprise.

"There is no way you can pin my father's death on me," she said. "We were reconciled some weeks ago."

"Yet you claimed not to have been in contact with him for several years," Alison quickly pointed out.

Rachel, realizing her mistake, looked confused.

"Well?" George Mason asked.

"My alibi is watertight," she adamantly asserted. "I was at The Pendle Inn, Longridge, lunching with my uncle on April 11th."

"Even if the waiter at The Three Fishes, Great Mytton could identify you as a lunch guest along with your father, whom he identified from a passport photograph, and a second, younger male, whom we can now assume was your uncle?"

Rachel Slade cast her eyes downwards, but said nothing. Behrens had obviously not kept his word regarding client confidentiality. So much for Swiss banking secrecy, she mused. And how on earth had this detective recovered her father's passport?

"This is just a preliminary interview, Mrs. Slade," Alison said. "We are not pressing any charges at this stage, but we must ask you to surrender your passport."

The jeweler reached in a drawer of her desk, where she had placed the document following her recent trip to Switzerland, and reluctantly handed it to her.

"We have no further questions at this stage," Mason then said.

"I have nothing to hide," the other said, vehemently. "I have a business to run, if you will permit me to do so."

"I have no problem with that," George Mason replied, stepping towards the shop door. "For the time being."

Once outside, the two detectives re-crossed Talbot Square and headed towards the promenade. The clock dial on the red-brick town hall registered 2.15 p.m.

"Time to grab a bite to eat," he remarked. "Haven't had a thing since breakfast."

"I'm hungry too," Alison said. "Must be the sea air."

"Getting the Blackpool bug already?" he teased.

"For a southerner like me," she responded, lightly, "it would more likely be the Clacton-on-Sea bug."

Having negotiated the busy tramway, George Mason directed

their steps towards North Pier, a sturdy Victorian structure reaching two hundred yards out into the Irish Sea. The tide was turning and they paused to watch the incoming breakers crash against its sturdy wooden supports.

"They do a first-rate fish-and-chips at the end of the pier," Mason said. "The fish comes fresh from Fleetwood, a little way up the coast."

"Suits me," Alison replied. "I love really fresh fish. It can be days old in supermarkets."

"An advantage of being on the coast," he replied.

Their seaward walk took them past amusements, ice cream vendors, souvenir booths, trinket stalls and the like to the bracing open-air restaurant at the far end. They took their seats above the sound of the waves. Raucous seagulls circled overhead, almost drowning out the piped pop music.

"So what was the main thing we learned just now?" Mason asked his companion, soon as they had placed their order.

"You mean, apart from the fact that you really put her on the spot?"

"Always with your assistance, Alison."

"We confirmed what we had suspected, from your conversation with that bank manager in Basel...what was his name, again?"

"Maurice Behrens."

"We confirmed that Rachel Slade knew all along of her father's death, for the simple reason that she was complicit in it."

Mason nodded in agreement.

"What else did we learn?" he asked, amiably.

Alison Aubrey averted her gaze towards the gulls perched on the pier railing, on the look-out for food. When diners threw scraps into the air, they swooped on them with unerring accuracy.

"They're scavengers," Mason said, with mock-disapproval. "They eat anything and everything."

"Beautiful creatures, none the less," Alison said. "So what else did we learn, George? You're the expert."

George Mason ignored the gentle sarcasm in her tone of voice and said:

"We now know the owner of the single cuff-link found near Seifert's body."

"The monogram R.M.?"

"Ralph Miller."

"Gosh, George, that's smart of you. I admit it hadn't occurred to me. So the daughter and her uncle must have been in cahoots?"

"It's certainly beginning to look that way," he replied, applying a dash of malt vinegar to his newly-served meal. "We'll be paying a visit to The Gables, Goosenargh, fairly soon."

Alison Aubrey also tucked into her fish-and-chips with good appetite. They both ate in silence for a while, enjoying a meal best eaten while it is still warm. The crying gulls and the cresting waves made for good company, reminding the senior detective of childhood visits to the coast, even if it had been Scarborough or Bridlington, favored by Yorkshire folk, rather than Blackpool or Fleetwood.

"Dessert?" he enquired, eventually.

"I'd like the apple-pie with vanilla ice-cream," Alison replied.

"Make it two, with coffee," Mason told the waitress hovering nearby, for once forgetting about his waistline.

"Do you think Ralph Miller was his original name?" Alison suddenly asked.

A wry smile played about her colleague's lips as the import of her question sank in.

"I mean, there has been a deal of name-changing in this case," the young sergeant continued.

"Heinrich Feldman became Heini Seifert," Mason said.

"Johann Mueller became John Miller."

"And Beate Mueller became Betty Miller!"

"Which makes Ralph Miller…?"

George Mason brought his palm down heavily onto the table.

"By Jove, Alison," he said. "You may have hit the jackpot!"

"…Rolf Mueller?"

"Brother of Celine Mueller/Miller."

"I'll get on to Bill Harrington right away."

With that, George Mason rose from his seat and crossed to the railing where, out of earshot of fellow diners, he placed a call to London on his cell-phone.

"Harrington," came the terse reply.

"George Mason here, Chief Inspector. Can you send someone over to Somerset House this afternoon, to find out if a German called Rolf Mueller changed his name by deed poll on arrival in this country, at some point in the early nineties?"

"That may be difficult, Inspector, at such short notice," his superior replied. "All personnel are fully stretched."

"This is extremely important," Mason said, imparting urgency to his voice. "Something of a breakthrough, as a result of our visit to Slade Jewelry."

"So where are you now?" the other testily enquired. "Sunning yourselves on Blackpool beach, more than likely."

George Mason ignored the jibe.

"Can you get someone over there first thing tomorrow morning?" he asked. "You can reach me at The Shireburn Arms, where we'll be spending the night."

"I'll make it a priority," Harrington said, more reasonably.

"That will be most helpful, Chief Inspector," Mason said, ending the call.

He returned to his table to rejoin Alison, who had already started on the dessert.

"Bill Harrington can't do anything until tomorrow morning," he told her. "But he will act on it first thing."

"That's big of him, George," she remarked, with uncharacteristic sarcasm.

"We'll just have to be patient," Mason replied. "It's about an hour by road from here to Whalley. Sergeant Wheeldon is driving over to meet us and take us back with him. He'll drop us off at our hotel, which is conveniently near his home."

"I'm looking forward to it," Alison said. "The Shireburn Arms sounds like a real country hotel."

"It must be a good place. Parents use it, I believe, when visiting their sons at Stonyhurst College."

"Isn't that the prominent Jesuit boarding-school one often reads about?"

"Indeed it is," her colleague replied. "I remember reading that Alfred Hitchcock and Arthur Conan Doyle were pupils there."

"No kidding, George?"

"And the famous poet Gerard Manley Hopkins taught classics there, in the late 1800s."

"Quite a cachet," Alison remarked. "Didn't he write *The Wreck of the Deutschland?*"

"The long poem about nuns who perished at sea after their expulsion from Germany under the Falk Laws? I believe he did."

"I read parts of it at school. But I prefer his nature poems, such as *The Windhover* and *Pied Beauty.*"

"Good choices, Alison. You've got good taste in literature."

"I majored in it at college," came the diffident reply.

Later that afternoon, a casually dressed Roy Wheeldon showed up, meeting the detectives at the pier by pre-arrangement. George Mason, to greet him properly, immediately bought a round of drinks at one of the pier bars.

"Good of you to help us out like this," he said.

"Don't mention it, Inspector," Wheeldon replied. "It's my day off and I've been intending to visit my mother for the past several weeks. She's living at a retirement home in Lytham St. Anne's."

"A smaller resort just down the coast," Mason explained, in reply to Alison's questioning look.

"I prefer it to Blackpool," Roy Wheeldon said. "It's much quieter and more refined. No amusement arcades, slot machines and similar tourist junk."

"I take your point, Sergeant," Mason said.

When they had finished their drinks, Roy Wheeldon led them to his car, parked across the way near Talbot Square. Once clear of the sprawling town, whose suburbs were favored by retirees from the industrial centers farther inland, he avoided the more direct route in favor of the minor roads leading across-country. As they approached the village of Goosenargh, George Mason asked him to find a parking spot, which he soon succeeded in doing directly opposite the medieval hall.

"That's Goosenargh Hall," the local officer said, "claimed to be the most haunted building in Britain."

The Scotland Yard pair regarded it with some astonishment and keen interest.

"That's amazing," Alison Aubrey said.

"Would you spend a night alone there?" Roy Wheeldon asked.

"Not for a thousand pounds," she emphatically replied.

"Just ghost stories," George Mason dismissively observed.

Leaving the car, a roomy Honda sedan, they strolled along the main street until they came to a large detached house.

"So this is The Gables," Mason said, weighing up the exterior, overgrown with ivy.

"Ralph Miller's address," Alison added. "Should we knock?"

"I think that may be a little premature," her colleague replied, "until we have heard back from Bill Harrington. What strikes you about this place, Alison?"

"There's a CHIROPRACTOR sign over the window."

"That struck me at once, too."

"So?" Alison asked.

"Chiropractic is a form of therapy," Mason said, "involving manipulation of the spinal column and other bone structures."

Light dawned across the young sergeant's features. She gave her colleague a long, admiring glance before saying, with a sly smile:

"A broken neck?"

Chapter Ten

At eleven o'clock the next day, Sergeant Roy Wheeldon, on receiving a telephone call from George Mason, left Whalley Police Station to drive the few miles to The Shireburn Arms, in the village of Hurst Green. Mason had earlier been in touch with Bill Harrington, who had that morning sent a junior officer over to Somerset House, where the nation's vital statistics were recorded. The official there had confirmed something Mason had recently begun to suspect, namely that Ralph Miller was called Rolf Mueller on arrival in England. In common with his parents, he had changed his name by deed poll soon afterwards. The senior detective had lingered over breakfast and read *The Times*, mainly for the cricket reports, while awaiting the call from London. Alison Aubrey had visited a local spa for therapeutic massage. They had spent the previous evening exploring the bucolic environs of Stonyhurst College and the River Ribble, before entertaining Roy Wheeldon and his wife to dinner at the hotel. They now stood by the hotel entrance as the local officer's car drew up and were soon on their way back to Goosenargh.

On arrival, Wheeldon parked his squad car outside the

chiropractor's and accompanied the two detectives inside. The receptionist reacted in surprise at the sight of a uniformed police officer and promptly summoned her employer from the adjoining surgery. Ralph Miller, dressed in a white tunic, appeared in the doorway with a questioning look on his intelligent features. He was a well-built man, whom Mason estimated to be around fifty years of age.

"Is there a problem?" Miller asked, thinking that perhaps he had collected a parking citation.

"Ralph Miller?" George Mason enquired.

The man nodded.

"I answer to that name," he replied.

"Inspector George Mason, from Scotland Yard," the detective said, producing ID. "I am arresting you on suspicion of involvement in the murder of Dr. Heini Seifert."

The chiropractor looked stunned and took a step backwards. His receptionist gave a cry of dismay.

"You can't be serious!" he exclaimed.

"I must ask you to accompany us to Whalley Police Station, for questioning."

"But there must be some mistake," Miller blustered.

"You will have ample opportunity to prove that in due course," Mason said, as Sergeant Wheeldon hand-cuffed him and led him outside, after he had given his receptionist hurried instructions about upcoming appointments. The two detectives then removed the computer hard-drive and followed the others to the waiting car. Less than an hour later, they were back in Whalley, where Wheeldon took charge of the computer, while the Mason and Aubrey confronted Miller in the interview room.

"Now please tell me what all this is about," the chiropractor said, adamantly.

George Mason showed him the cuff-link with the monogram R.M.

"Do you recognize this?" he asked.

Ralph Miller's eyes narrowed.

"It could belong to anybody," he said.

"It was found close to Dr. Seifert's body at Whalley Nab on the morning of April 12th last."

Miller merely shrugged, looking unconcerned.

"Let me state my case," Mason then said. "Your original name was Rolf Mueller. You were born at Dresden, in the German Democratic Republic. Soon after reunification in 1991, you moved to this country, changing your name to Ralph Miller."

A look of surprised amusement spread across the other's features.

"You have done your homework, Inspector," he said. "All of this is true, but how does this relate to Dr. Seifert's death?"

"In this way," Mason replied. "Heini Seifert's birth name was Heinrich Feldman. He acted as an informer for the East German secret police, known as the Stasi. One of the people he informed on was your father, Reverend Johann Mueller, who as a result received a long prison sentence."

Ralph Miller's look changed to one of amazement.

"How could you possibly have unearthed all this?" he asked.

"Routine detective work," Mason blandly replied. "And I am putting it to you that this was sufficient motive for murder, as an act of revenge."

"Purely circumstantial evidence," the other scoffed. "It would never hold up in court."

"He's right, George," Alison Aubrey said. "We need more than this."

"And I suspect we shall get it," Mason retorted, "once the experts have examined the computer."

"Sergeant Wheeldon is making arrangements for that, at Lancashire Constabulary HQ in Preston," Alison said. "It will take time."

"One thing has long puzzled me about this case," Mason then said, addressing the chiropractor. "Why would your sister Celine have married Heinrich Feldman, aka Heini Seifert, knowing what he did to your father?"

"She would not necessarily have known," Ralph Miller replied. "Informers always acted under the radar, to protect themselves. And even if Celine had known, she may not have held it against Feldman. People were brain-washed, Inspector, by intensive propaganda, into unquestioning loyalty to the regime. She may well have thought that father had erred."

"I would prefer to think that she was not aware of her husband's activities," Alison said.

"You're entitled to your own view of the matter," Miller replied, with a glance of ironic amusement towards the young detective. "It makes no difference to anything now. All water under the bridge. My sister Celine is dead, my father and mother are both dead."

"And you are being held on suspicion of murder."

* * *

Three days later, following the weekend after his return to London, Chief Inspector Harrington called George Mason into his office. They sat facing each other across the unusually tidy walnut desk.

"I gather you had a useful fishing expedition up north," Bill Harrington said, evidently in buoyant mood.

"Detective Sergeant Aubrey and I made good progress," Mason replied. "We interviewed Rachel Slade and arrested her uncle, Ralph Miller, on suspicion of murder. He was transferred over the weekend to Wormwood Scrubs."

"Where he'll be quite comfortable for the time being," the other drily remarked. "Now I have some news for you."

An administrative assistant brought in a pot of coffee at that point, causing Harrington's right hand to hover momentarily in the vicinity of his whiskey drawer, but for some reason he refrained.

"I had a call from Klaas Hendrijks first thing this morning," he said. "The Kommandant informed me that Ivo Grigorev has already been apprehended."

"How so soon?" Mason queried, agreeably surprised at the speed of events.

"He was spotted at the Romanian border," Harrington explained. "Hendrijks put out an alert through Interpol. A lucky break, in a way, since one can travel through most of Europe, in the so-called Schengen Area, without a passport these days."

"But Romania is not part of Schengen?" Mason asked, cottoning on.

"Exactly. His quite valid passport gave him away. He's now in custody in Bucharest. Hendrijks thinks he could be part of the Omega Network the Dutch police have been trying to penetrate for quite some time. Grigorev's arrest is a major breakthrough for them."

"Glad to hear it," George Mason said, "if it shuts down their operation in England."

"It will certainly set them back for a good spell, but no doubt they will eventually recover. These people seem to have endless resources...as well as finance."

"The Clitheroe facility is defunct, at least," Mason informed him. "The real estate company is, according to Sergeant Wheeldon, in the process of re-letting the premises, to a dentist, of all people."

"Poetic irony," Harrington quipped.

"What about the young Serb, Zivko Plesijc?"

"Deported."

"Just like that?"

"Afraid so," an unsympathetic Bill Harrington replied. "Now, there have been developments in the Miller case. The Lancashire police worked overtime during the weekend to extract e-mail exchanges between Ralph Miller and his niece, Rachel Slade. It's all in this file."

He passed a large Manila folder across the desk.

"Go directly to the Scrubs, Inspector. You can read this material on the way. Now I have a meeting with the Superintendent, if you will excuse me."

The two officers rose from their seats simultaneously to leave the office. George Mason gave a thumbs-up sign to Alison Aubrey, who was in the general office doing routine deskwork, before leaving the Yard. In a buoyant frame of mind, he crossed Whitehall towards Westminster Underground Station, where he took the District Line tube to Hammersmith. On alighting, he walked the short distance to the prison and passed through its storied portal. Ralph Miller was summoned to meet him in the interview room. After a weekend in the Scrubs, he was much less self-assured.

"The Lancashire police have examined your computer," Mason informed him. "I have the transcripts with me here."

He placed the contents of the Manila folder on the desk, reading from each item in turn.

"Rachel Slade states that she has arranged for you both to join her father for lunch at The Three Fishes, Great Mytton, at 1.30 p.m. on April 11th."

"I don't dispute that."

"You niece in fact lied about it. She told me the lunch was at The Pendle Inn, Longridge, several miles away."

Ralph Miller shifted position uneasily.

"The ostensible purpose of the lunch was to complete a reconciliation between Rachel and her father. Your e-mail in response to that was an enquiry as to whether Dr. Seifert had made a new will, naming your niece as sole beneficiary."

The chiropractor noticeably winced.

"The next item is even more compromising, Mr. Miller," George Mason said. "Rachel says that no one could now connect you with your past life in Dresden, since you altered your name on arrival in England. She also said that nobody could possibly suspect your motive."

"It is true that both my parents and I altered our names," Miller said.

"You then suggest Whalley Nab as a good place to take your brother-in-law for the afternoon. Dr. Seifert was a keen hiker and would readily have accepted that suggestion. Rachel's reply to that was the single word 'Accident?' I take that to mean she was setting up an incident that could easily look like an accident, in the shape of a fall from the Nab. I put it to you, Mr. Miller, that Dr. Seifert did not suffer a fall, but that you used your professional skills as a chiropractor to break his neck, after conspiring with your niece to lure her father to Whalley on the pretext of completing the reconciliation."

The chiropractor stared stonily back at his interviewer for several minutes before saying, with a resigned look:

"You seem to have all the answers, Inspector Mason," he said, "except for one."

"I take it that Rachel's motive for murder was to acquire control of her father's estate," the detective said. "But I am not sure what your motive could be, if not also for financial gain."

"It's more complicated than that," the other said.

"Can you elaborate on that?"

Ralph Miller cleared his throat and took a glass of water from the flask provided.

"Both Rachel and I," he said, "considered my brother-in-law responsible for Celine's death."

"I read the transcript of the trial," Mason said. "You did not agree with the verdict?"

"Absolutely not," came the emphatic reply. "Seifert was my sister's physician, responsible for regulating the medication."

"You are implying that Seifert over-prescribed," the detective asked, "counter to the trial verdict that Celine deliberately over-dosed as a result of her depression?"

"That is my view of the matter."

"You seem very convinced, but on what grounds?"

"Not long before this tragic event took place," Miller continued, "my sister sent me a letter outlining her suspicions of her husband's activities at Wellman Clinic."

"You mean she suspected him of performing illegal organ transplants?"

The chiropractor nodded.

"At the time, I was deployed oversees with the Army Medical Corps. Her letter did not reach me until after the trial. When I finally received it, on my return to England, I approached the Crown Prosecution Service to stage a re-trial in this country, on the grounds that her husband had silenced her to cover up his illegal activities, which were, as you can probably appreciate, very lucrative."

"With what result?" an intrigued George Mason asked.

"They refused, quoting the principle of Double Jeopardy."

"You mean that, having been found not guilty in the Swiss court, Seifert could not be re-tried here for the same incident?"

"Exactly."

George Mason, pouring himself a glass of water, sat back in his chair to take stock of this surprising new development. It was several minutes before he said:

"So what you and your niece Rachel Slade did, in effect, was to take the law into your own hands and make Heini Seifert pay in full for his putative crime?"

Ralph Miller returned an ironic smile.

"He received his just desserts," he said, simply. "I was determined that he would not profit by Celine's death."

"There will certainly be a new trial," Mason then said. "But it will be you and Rachel Slade in the dock."

Miller emitted a heavy sigh.

"So be it," he replied, resignedly.

"One more thing puzzles me," the detective then said.

"Fire away," the other replied.

"In view of the suspicions your sister Celine raised about

Wellman Clinic, why did you not then approach the health authorities regarding them?"

"Oh, I did indeed do so," Miller said. "I wrote to the Ministry of Health about the matter, soon after the Crown Prosecution Service turned down my request for a second trial."

"With what result?"

"They informed me, after an interval of several weeks, that they would send an inspector over to Clitheroe to look into the matter. That was the last I heard about it. All I do know is that my brother-in-law ran the clinic until the day before his death."

George Mason reacted in amazement.

"Sounds like a cover-up," he remarked, "involving a corrupt official. There was a similar case recently in East Europe, where health ministry personnel issued permits to a clinic performing illegal kidney transplants. I never imagined it could happen here, and I shall certainly have Scotland Yard look into it further."

"Take it as you will, Inspector," Miller replied. "It's no longer my concern."

George Mason rose from his chair to signify an end to the interview.

"I advise you to get in touch with a good lawyer, Mr. Miller," he said, finally. "Meanwhile, we shall be taking out a warrant for Rachel Slade's arrest."

+ + +

Zivko Plesijc relaxed in the comfort of a second-class compartment of the Rotterdam-Innsbruck express, dubbed *Erasmus* after the famous 16th Century humanist, and watched the rows of tenements slip by, wondering what had become of Ivo and Marika Grigorev, who owned an apartment in the port city. He reflected on the recent course of events, how he had been driven to Longsight, Manchester, only to discover that Anna Nikolic had moved on; how he had approached the Salvation Army at the suggestion of the landlady of The White Hart and been betrayed to the authorities. Things had gone reasonably well after that, all things considered. The supervisor of Irlam Detention Center had eventually procured the services of an interpreter, enabling him to tell his story in full. People were sympathetic, viewing him as a victim of unscrupulous agents, and had succeeded in tracing Anna through the National Health Service. To his immense joy and relief, he had been able to speak to her by telephone and hear the sound of her voice. The upshot of this belated contact was that Anna was committed to serve the remainder of her one-year contract with the NHS, who had paid her expenses to Britain. After that, in a few months' time, she would return to Belgrade and seek employment there based on her valuable experience in the UK.

The prospect of their settling down together on home turf greatly comforted the young Serb, as the train left the environs of the city and struck out across the flat Dutch landscape. The *Erasmus* would reach Innsbruck by evening, with a connection to Vienna, where he would take the overnight sleeper service to Belgrade. A quick deportation was about the last thing he anticipated when he had embarked on this adventure several weeks ago, after meeting the man he knew only as Fedor, who had arranged for him to meet with Ivo Grigorev. But he did not feel ill-done-by. He was physically intact and the British authorities had generously provided him with a rail ticket home. He bore the Grigorevs no ill-will, recalling with affection Marika's efforts to improve his English. And he had visited the home of that most storied of English soccer clubs, Manchester United. How envious his friends in Belgrade would be of that!